TELLING STORIES
VOLUME 2

To Rachel,
Don't just read your
clients...

Love, D.

March '93

Also edited by Duncan Minshull,
and available from Coronet:

TELLING STORIES

including stories by:
A. L. BARKER
MAEVE BINCHY
CHRISTOPHER BURNS
MICHAEL CARSON
ANGELA CARTER
MARY FLANAGAN
JANE GARDAM
ROMESH GUNESEKERA
CHRISTOPHER HOPE
JOHN McGAHERN
DEBORAH MOGGACH
RICHARD NELSON
FREDERIC RAPHAEL
MICHELE ROBERTS
DILYS ROSE
GREG SNOW
D. J. TAYLOR
JONATHAN TREITEL
LYNNE TRUSS

Telling Stories
Volume 2

The best of BBC Radio's recent short fiction

Edited by Duncan Minshull

Title story by Russell Hoban

CORONET
Hodder and Stoughton

This collection first published in Great Britain in 1993 as a Coronet paperback original

Introduction and compilation copyright © 1992 Duncan Minshull

For copyright on individual stories see page v

The characters and situations in this book are entirely imaginary and bear no relation to any real person or actual happenings.

The right of the contributors to be identified as the authors of this work has been asserted by them in accordance with the Copyright, Designs and Patents Act 1988.

This book is sold subject to the condition that it shall not, by way of trade or otherwise, be lent, re-sold, hired out or otherwise circulated without the publisher's prior consent in any form of binding or cover other than that in which it is published and without a similar condition including this condition being imposed on the subsequent purchaser.

No part of this publication may be reproduced or transmitted in any form or by any means, electronic or mechanical, including photocopying, recording or any information storage or retrieval system, without either the prior permission in writing from the publisher or a licence, permitting restricted copying. In the United Kingdom such licences are issued by the Copyright Licensing Agency, 90 Tottenham Court Road, London W1P 9HE.

British Library CIP

A CIP catalogue record for this title is available from the British Library

ISBN 0-340-58349-5

Printed and bound in Great Britain for Hodder and Stoughton Paperbacks, a division of Hodder and Stoughton Ltd, Mill Road, Dunton Green, Sevenoaks, Kent TN13 2YA. (Editorial Office: 47 Bedford Square, London WC1B 3DP) by Clays Ltd, St Ives plc, Bungay, Suffolk. Photoset by Rowland Phototypesetting Ltd, Bury St Edmunds, Suffolk.

ACKNOWLEDGEMENTS

BEYOND THE BLUE MOUNTAINS copyright © 1992 by
  Penelope Lively
TO TEMPT A WOMAN copyright © 1993 by Clare
  Boylan
HAVE YOU HAD A NICE DAY? copyright © 1993 by
  Francis King
PASTORAL copyright © 1993 by David Lodge
BLAME IT ON THE PILGRIMS copyright © 1993 by
  Anne Leaton
LA BELLE DAME SANS 'THINGWY' copyright © 1993
  by Liz Lochhead
MEN FRIENDS copyright © 1993 by Angela Huth
A MINE OF SERPENTS copyright © 1993 by Shena
  Mackay
RABBITS copyright © 1993 by Lawrence Scott
CRYING, TALKING, SLEEPING, WALKING copyright ©
  1993 by Greg Snow
LEAVING DOYLE'S CROSS copyright © 1993 by Frank
  Ronan
COWBOYS copyright © 1993 by Stephen Amidon
THE RAILINGS copyright © 1993 by Ronald Frame
THE DEATH OF THE ELMS copyright © 1993 by
  Georgina Hammick
THE LUNCH BOX copyright © 1993 by Gillian Tindall
BRAHMS INTERMEZZO (NR 118) copyright © 1993 by
  Irene Dische
ABROAD copyright © 1993 by Peter Regent
ICE DANCING copyright © 1993 by Rose Tremain
THE INTERVIEW copyright © 1993 by Maeve Binchy
TELLING STORIES copyright © 1993 by Russell Hoban

CONTENTS

INTRODUCTION

A year on from the publication of Telling Stories (1) and another three hundred short stories have been broadcast on BBC Radio, often to audiences reaching half a million ... Quite a literary gathering: making us the largest patron of short fiction in the country. So, from such a rich seam come the twenty stories that make up book number two. New pieces that should prove as persuasive on the page as they were when heard on Radio 4's Short Story programme, or on Radio 3, before and after various evening concerts.

And the selection? Certainly stories that appear for the first time in book form. And, importantly, from a range of voices: I am delighted that Rose Tremain, Shena Mackay, Penelope Lively and Clare Boylan all accepted commissions; I am delighted that the playwright Liz Lochhead has her first-ever story included; Russell Hoban has written the title-story; and there is an intriguing mix of newer names to announce – Irene Dische, Frank Ronan, Stephen Amidon, Lawrence Scott and Peter Regent.

Themes and preoccupations are explored in abundance. There are stories celebratory and sceptical of Christmas, Easter, Guy Fawkes and American Thanksgiving. And most refreshing is the impulse to get away from what is local: writing for radio lets you paint a picture of anywhere and everywhere – so why be content with the back-yard. On offer are snaps of mid-America, the Australian bush, the Himalayas, India and provincial Japan.

But if you failed to visit these and other places at the time of broadcast, then I hope that the version in print will be just as enjoyable.

Good reading!

Duncan Minshull
Short Story Editor, BBC Radio

BEYOND THE BLUE MOUNTAINS

Penelope Lively

Penelope Lively was born and grew up in Egypt. She now lives in London and Oxfordshire. She is the author of nine novels, a number of children's books and several collections of short stories. Her novel *Moon Tiger* won the Booker Prize in 1987. Her new novel is published this spring.

'Beyond The Blue Mountains' was commissioned with *Traveller Magazine* and broadcast on Radio 4. The reader was Hannah Gordon.

BEYOND THE BLUE MOUNTAINS

Myra and George Purbeck, aboard the *Empress of Sydney*, rode through the Hawkesbury River valley. The *Empress of Sydney* was a coach, of an extravagance that neither had ever before experienced – a double-decker with picture windows of tinted glass, luxuriantly upholstered seating and small tilted movie screens lest the voyager should weary of the landscape. From time to time a stewardess plied them with coffee or freshly squeezed orange juice. The air conditioning was just right; the restful and uninsistent background music was interrupted periodically by a voice which delivered a laconic, informative and sometimes witty account of the passing scene. They had been given a run-down of the social composition of suburban Sydney, with a digression on architectural style. They had learned about the crops grown in the farmland through which they now passed and about breeds of cattle and of sheep. 'Look left and you'll see three black swans on a billabong. The black swan is native to Australia.' Myra listened with interest.

She said 'Is it the driver who does this commentary, do you imagine?'

'Presumably.' George was reading – intermittently – a copy of the London *Financial Times*. He was also, of course, gathering strength for the next leg of an exacting business trip. It was Sunday. The coach trip was for Myra's benefit: a kindly indulgence.

In Sydney, while George performed business, she had wandered at first jet-lagged and punch-drunk. She felt as though she had stepped into an alternative universe.

The birds that flew in the garden of their hotel were little parrots, she saw with astonishment. The trees and shrubs were eerie and beautiful developments of familiar trees and shrubs. The very air seemed different. Then she had gone into an art gallery and seen on the walls a further miraculous transformation of the known world. The paintings showed a brilliant landscape, vibrant with colour – blues and golds and a bright ochre, a place of rock and dust and tree that was vast, bold and disturbing. Some of the pictures were of forest scenes. They depicted dappled light, sparkling water and exuberant growth. In one, an aborigine family camped around a fire in a clearing. Wallabies grazed, the trees were roped with flowering vines, shafts of light fell on emerald grass. Myra gazed in fascination; words she did not normally use flew into her head – a glade, an arcadian glade. Emerging once more into the heat and sunshine of the city, she was elated. The jet-lag faded. She began to feel unusually alert and well.

In the evenings they dined with business associates of George's, who asked her what she thought of Oz and then moved on to other matters without listening to her answer. George smiled benignly and sometimes he replied on her behalf, saying that Myra was having a fine old time in the shopping malls. He had brought her on this trip because she was on his conscience.

The coach began to climb. They had left the farmland behind and were entering the foothills of the Blue Mountains. The Blue Mountains, explained the invisible commentator, are thus named because of the sun's effect on the haze of oil vapour given off by eucalyptus trees.

At the beginning of the nineteenth century they formed an impenetrable barrier between the expanding settlement and the hinterland beyond, until the pioneering expedition of Blaxland, Lawson and Wentworth in 1813 which led to the construction within six months of the first road through the mountains by hand-picked convict labourers.

Myra looked through the rose-tinted windows of the *Empress of Sydney* at the steep slopes, the rock, the soaring trees. The coach, now, swung around hairpin bends.

She said 'Six months . . . It's incredible.'

4

George was busy with his laptop. He lifted his eyes and stared for a few moments out of the window. He became reflective. Myra doubted that his thoughts were on Blaxland, Lawson and Wentworth or, indeed, the convicts.

The coach was sparsely populated. Up here on the top deck there were six immaculately suited Japanese who sat together in a cluster, a couple of backpacking American girls, and a waste of empty seats. The commentator began to talk of flora and fauna. He told the passengers to look for tree ferns, for casuarinas and for sulphur-crested cockatoos. When they reached the viewpoint and the revolving restaurant they must take a stroll and listen for bell-birds. If anyone had any questions feel free to hand a note to the stewardess.

Myra tore a page out of her diary. She wrote 'What are the scarlet flowers on low bushes?' She gave it to the stewardess.

Five minutes later, the coach drew up at the roadside. Myra, looking down through the window, saw a lanky figure drop from the driver's compartment and vanish into the undergrowth of the steep hillside. A minute later he reappeared, leapt back up into the coach. They moved off once more. 'In fifteen minutes or so we shall reach the famous viewpoint, where you have a two hour stop to enjoy the wonderful views beyond the Blue Mountains. Take a ride across the valley on the funicular railway, have a walk in the bush but be careful to stick to the paths – easy to get lost in this country. And you'll get a fine three course meal in the revolving restaurant. Have a good time. And for the passenger who's interested in flowers – it's red honey-flower. Mountain Devil, we call it.'

The stewardess had arrived at Myra's elbow. She held out a tray on which was perched a spray of silky scarlet flowers. 'With the driver's compliments.'

Myra picked up the flowers. 'Thank you.' She tucked them into the top buttonhole of her shirt. She felt a surge of gaiety, a swoop of well-being which exactly matched the exuberance of the blossoms.

They arrived at their destination – a complex of cafés and restaurants at the highest point of the mountain range. The various viewpoints looked out across an apparently endless sequence of blue-green ridges splashed here and there with the rich brown of a rock face. Myra, alighting from the coach, was again seized with exhilaration. This place is doing something to me, she thought. It was as though she had shed a skin, and stepped out new-minted and charged with life.

There were the restaurants, and the ticket office for the funicular railway which swooped dizzyingly down over the mountain-side. And there all around them beyond the car-park were stretches of dappled woodland that made her think at once of that painting. She saw tree ferns, with grey scaly trunks and a brilliant eruption of bracken-like leaves. She saw the ropes of flowering creepers, the bright grass on which quivered gold coins of sunlight. She looked for grazing wallabies, and a tranquil aborigine family.

'Let's go for a walk.'

But George preferred to sit on the restaurant terrace with a beer. He had some phone calls to make, too. Ah yes, thought Myra, no doubt. 'Fine,' she said. 'I'll walk for a bit and come back for lunch. In this revolving restaurant, I suppose.'

She visited the toilets, and then set off. She chose a narrow path which looked the least frequented, and followed it into the trees. And instantly she heard a bell-bird – a clear sweet chiming sound from some invisible presence high in the waving branches.

The trees thinned out. There was a clearing. And there in the clearing, leaned up against a rock reading a newspaper, with a sandwich in one hand and a can of Coke alongside, was a man. A long, rangy man in ubiquitous Aussie gear – shirt, shorts and knee-socks. Myra prepared to walk tactfully past.

He looked up. 'Hi, there. Enjoying the trip?'

She put two and two together. Of course. The driver.

'I certainly am. And thank you for the flowers.'

'My pleasure.'

She had slowed up only very slightly. Now she was alongside him, and starting to move away.

6

'Take care,' he said. 'Stick to the path.'

'I will,' said Myra. 'And I heard a bell-bird.'

'Great.' He was looking directly at her and the look, she suddenly saw, was one of appreciation, genial and in no way offensive. I like what I see, it said. Maybe we could have got together, under other circumstances.

He raised his paper. She walked on.

Well, thought Myra. Well.

She was not a vain woman, never had been. She saw herself, objectively, as the sort of person who is not much noticed. Unassertive. This, perhaps, accounted for much.

And now, here, in this interesting other world, she felt different. And, it would seem, appeared differently.

The path looped round in a circle and returned her to the car-park and to the restaurant terrace. She cruised in, walking tall, hungry, brisk and seeing everything very sharp and clear. Her husband, sitting there with his laptop, his newspaper and his beer.

They sat opposite one another in the revolving restaurant. Myra chose a seafood salad, avoiding the Filet of Buffalo with Confit of Beetroot. George ate a steak, medium rare.

They spoke, briefly, of arrangements for the following day, of a handbag Myra had purchased for her sister, of a difficulty George was experiencing with his computer. Myra told him of the bell-bird.

She spoke of other birds she had noticed – the rosellas in the hotel garden, a kookaburra on a gatepost by the roadside. As she talked she saw the mountain ranges inch slowly past George's head. They sat within a creeping sphere, a dramatic and sumptuous backcloth quite at odds with the clatter of knives and forks, the red checked napery and the chomping diners. Myra's sense of disorientation became acute. Disorientation, and a certain wild confidence.

George was not listening to her. He was looking beyond her left shoulder. His eyes were blank. She knew what he was thinking about. He was thinking about Bridget Cashell, his mistress.

7

She said, 'You're thinking about Bridget Cashell, your mistress, aren't you?'

Mistress. She relished the word. It had overtones of satin dressing-gowns. Bridget Cashell was in fact accounts manager in George's firm and although distinctly personable was not at all the satin dressing-gown type. Myra listened to her own words with astonishment and satisfaction.

George too listened, apparently. His eyes leapt to life. Myra saw surprise, dismay, and a process of rapid thought:

'I didn't realise you knew, Myra.' He had rejected prevarication, it seemed.

'Oh, yes.'

She thought, and what's more, all of a sudden, out here, I know that I don't really love you any more. She watched him. He looked away. He pushed his food aside, the food uneaten.

'Did you get her on the phone all right, just now?'

'It's the middle of the night, in England.'

'Of course – how silly of me. You could try this evening.'

'Please, Myra.'

They sat in silence for a while. Myra finished her seafood salad, which was excellent. Many times, back home, in that other world where it was the middle of the night, she had thought about having this conversation but it had never, in the head, been at all like this.

'Myra . . .' he began.

She picked up the menu. 'Do you want a dessert? I'm having tropical fruit salad. Papaya, guava . . . What's paw-paw, do you know?'

He shook his head. 'Myra, I'm finding it hard to know what to say . . .'

'Never mind,' she said quite kindly. 'You've had a shock.'

She observed him. Behind his head, the Blue Mountains smoothly revolved. His face had a shrivelled look; he sat hunched into his chair. It occurred to Myra that he had become slightly smaller within the last few minutes. He was a big man normally, who sat erect.

Her next words rose quite unconsidered to her lips. 'Do you want to get rid of me and marry her?'

As soon as she had spoken she saw that she had hit the jackpot. George's eyes were eloquent with panic.

'No. No, Myra. Absolutely not. The last thing I . . . Look, should we talk about all this here? Wouldn't it be better if we sit down quietly back at the hotel . . . Or maybe when we get home to England, when we've both had a chance to think a bit.'

'I've been thinking,' said Myra. 'Quite a bit, really. But you may be right. We'll leave it, then. Sure you don't want any dessert?'

They finished the meal. Not in silence, for Myra chatted of the scenery and of their fellow eaters and George, wearing still this strange diminished look, responded wanly to her comments. He agreed that the Japanese were obsessed with photography. He turned to note the grove of casuarinas that she pointed out. On the walk back to the coach he listened – fruitlessly – for the bell-bird.

The driver stood by the door. He said to Myra, 'Hi, there,' and Myra smiled. The passengers resumed their seats, the coach started up and began the slow twisting descent down from the unfettered vistas of the mountain ranges and into the neat and structured universe of the Hawkesbury River valley and the wide road to Sydney. The commentary ceased. A movie came on; headphones were distributed.

George sat holding his newspaper, but did not turn the pages. And Myra saw now that they would not talk, either at the hotel or back home in England. What had passed between them today would remain for ever beyond the Blue Mountains, potent and powerful. She felt a touch sorry for Bridget Cashell. And possibly for George.

TO TEMPT A WOMAN

Clare Boylan

Clare Boylan is the author of four novels and two books of short stories. She is a regular contributor to Radio 4's Short Story Programme and her most recent novel is *Home Rule*. She lives in County Kildare, Ireland.

'To Tempt A Woman' was first broadcast on Radio 4, read by Tony Doyle.

TO TEMPT A WOMAN

The two old men entered Moran's Fashion House accompanied, unknown to themselves, by the ghosts of their lives. A rich spoor of dung and straw patterned the shop's royal blue carpet in the wake of their boots and there echoed off their insignificant persons surprising bass and alto notes from beer and whiskey, from dreams of women that made random raids on the derelict imagination, from linament and black tea and blood.

Miss Hartigan sighted the spectres before she registered their human catalysts. Her reaction was appropriate to the horror. She left off the cutting of a good wool broadcloth and rushed forward to defend her stock.

The old men gazed around the coats and corsets, the boots and bales of cloth, as they were in a foreign country and all the tribes spoke among themselves in a foreign language.

'Do ye want something?' Miss Hartigan still held the long-nosed shears. A measuring tape, snaked about her shoulders, seemed there to lay witness to the girth of her chest.

'Sure, we do,' they said. 'We'd like a fur coat.'

She saw them as a couple of bowsies, too addled to know where they had wandered in to. 'I'd like one too,' she sneered.

'We're not buyin' it for you,' they quickly assured her. 'Are you coddin'?'

'You want a fur?' She eyed the fabric of their overcoats, tweed that had developed a sheen as if something had chewed it.

'Here!' one old man said, understanding her. He pulled from his pocket a thick wad of dirty notes of money. The men studied with interest the set of teeth she displayed then,

13

not home grown but hard and white as lime. 'Mink or mus-quash?' she smiled.

'What squash?'

'That's like a turnip.'

'We wouldn't go for that.'

'How much is mink?'

When she told them they knew they were not in a foreign country but on another planet.

'There is opossum,' Miss Hartigan said.

Quids?' One old man rubbed his thumb and forefinger together, harsh in his fright. 'Name your price.' She named it and they reacted with ire. 'Do you think we're amadans?'

'Was there not another shaggin' creature on Noah's Ark?' 'Lynx, weasel, badger, stoat,' they tried to help her out.

She knew that male irritation could quickly turn to fury. She was familiar with the bilious strength of old men. Suits could be ripped and mirrors kicked to pieces. 'There is rabbit,' she said softly. At first she pronounced it as if she would neither eat nor wear it and then she forced her voice to sound pleasant. 'It's very nice. Also known as a coney or a fun fur. Twenty pounds,' she added. She waited, suspending her breath until they relaxed into their normal state of unease.

'We'd have to see it on.'

'Would you like me to try it on?'

This suggestion cheered them up. 'God, no! She's not a heifer.'

They pointed to a young girl who was behind a mysterious woman's counter labelled 'haberdashery'. Upon Miss Hartigan's signal the girl approached. She wore a white blouse with a fretwork of flowers on the collar.

Tod Cuddy imagined such a presence in his kitchen, her round little face pink from the heat of stove or washtub. Would she ever get used, he wondered, to the stream where at one point the butter churns were dipped for cooling and at another spot you had your wash and, far down where no one could see, you used the running water for a toilet?

He had only a son. It seemed a big thing, thirty years ago

when the boy was born. Now they couldn't see eye to eye at all. It had been assumed that when the lad grew up he would get married and take over the farm but he only wanted a TV. Since they got it, he had done nothing except sprawl at its screen watching black and white pictures of people blowing each others' brains out or having a go at each other in bed, taking longer over it than you'd take to eat your dinner. They spent their evenings in front of the telly, sitting in the cold kitchen. Occasionally Tadgh drove out to town for chips or an awful thing called a pissa. Tod was too long widowed now to be thinking of starting out with another woman but he did nine holy hours and went off the drink for the duration in the hopes that someone would fall for the lad. It would take a miracle.

Then the miracle had occurred. Tod Cuddy met a man called Ned Flavin who was trying to get rid of his daughter.

'Why doesn't she go out and get herself a guy like any normal girl?' Cuddy had cautiously enquired.

'Phena's only seventeen. She hasn't got around to that sort of thing.'

'Is she a swank? Is she used to finery?' Tod sharply interrogated.

'Get away. She hasn't a bean. She's a nice little thing. The nuns taught her to make a lovely brown soda. Mrs Flavin prefers a white sliced from the local Spar. Presents it at table as if she cut the slices with the cheeks of her backside.' His laugh came out as an unhappy growl. He couldn't tell a stranger why he had to get Phena married. He couldn't mention the letter from the nuns concerning his daughter. The mere thought of it filled him with rage.

Cuddy had approached his son that evening and proposed Phena Flavin to him in marriage. The lad did not remove his gaze from the screen but continued trying to catch with his mouth, the Tayto Crisps tossed from their bag by hand. 'Do you have any feelings in the matter?' Tod persevered. Tadgh shrugged.

'She's a nice little thing,' Cuddy coaxed. 'You'd want to shake yourself.'

'What do you mean?' The boy now turned from the entertainment, amazed.

'You'd be expected to have a fresh shirt at the ready and to clean your teeth regular.'

'My teeth are clent regular,' the boy protested. Menacingly he bared at his father his durable but unappealing fangs.

'So you're keen,' the father murmured, noting with gratitude that the screen had reclaimed the lad's attention.

When Cuddy met Phena Flavin he was taken aback. She wasn't a nice little thing as her father had said. The girl was a beauty. There were plenty of females that you'd look at in the town, grand big ones with their figures bursting out of their gansies, but this creature was of a different order. Perfection sat upon her the way it dìd on a primrose in a field.

'She could get any guy,' Tod burst out in fright.

'Of course we'd like to see her settled with a nice bit of land but we wouldn't ask her to do anything against her will, Mrs Flavin said. 'She'd have to be tempted.' Tod shook his head helplessly at the notion of Tadgh tempting anyone. 'We're not short of a bob,' he offered doubtfully. Mrs Flavin smiled to put him at his ease and offered a slice of Mother's Pride spread with Spar strawberry jam. She was only half her husband's age but there was coarseness about her that seemed to infect everything she touched and he couldn't eat the meal, thinking of what Flavin had said about the slicing of the bread.

When he was going, the girl got his greasy coat from the hall. 'Are you at school still?' he asked her quickly.

'I've done my Leaving,' she told him.

'I suppose you have big plans.'

'I'd like to go to the uni.' She blushed.

'Now, Miss!' Her father warned.

The old men had no ideas about tempting women. Neither of them respected Mrs Flavin's view in the matter. She would probably speak of gin or kisses. In the end Cuddy had the inspiration of speaking to the priest in confession. 'If a man wanted to tempt a woman, what item, failing himself, would render her helpless to resist?' The priest had answered without any hesitation that no woman born could withstand the provocation of a fur coat.

Now the mission was accomplished. The two men marched along the main street, grim with excitement, swinging the bag by its waxed string handles. They stopped suddenly and laughed out loud as if they had pulled off something daring, like a raid on a bank. 'A drink, man!' Flavin proposed. They could hear the fur coat languorously shifting in the bag, inside its undergarment of white tissue.

When several pints had worn the edges off his nerves, Cuddy found a question rising up in his mind and at last, like a burp, he had to let it out. 'Is it fair on the girl?'

He was thinking of having to tell her to bring her square of newspaper down to the stream. Would she remind him that this was 1967, that men had landed on the moon and the Beatles were selling in millions? In his mind the fur coat had already imbued her with a glamour that put her out of reach.

'You know nothing about the case,' Flavin rounded on him in a fury.

'What is it?' Cuddy was suddenly frightened. 'What are you trying to tell me? Is she used goods?'

'I've had a letter,' the other old man said bitterly. 'From a nun. Sister Felicity! Did you ever hear tell of a nun with a name like Felicity?'

Flavin fell into a thunderous silence and Cuddy wagged his head from side to side as if making a comment, although in fact it was embarrassment. Nothing more was said about the letter. He was shy in matters relating to women. At first he felt a profound disappointment that Phena was not as he had imagined her, but after he had taken several whiskies he was glad she had some awful bloody secret. Whenever he felt sorry for her he could think about that and hold it against her.

*

17

'I have to talk to you, Miss!'

Phena turned cautiously from her task at the table when she heard her father. She could tell from his voice that he had been drinking and when she met his eye she recognised the livid and bewildered look. 'I know,' she said, 'I know what it is.'

'What do you know?' Her father demanded.

'It's the letter. Sister Felicity told me.'

'It would be better if that matter was not mentioned at all,' the old man warned.

'She told me,' Phena burst out. She could not contain her excitement. A light seemed to shine through her face from somewhere inside her. 'She has a past pupil in America who needs a bright girl to look after her children. Sister Felicity said that I was her brightest star. The woman will pay for me to go to college.'

'You want to go?'

'Oh, Daddy, I do.'

'America!' Flavin spat on the ground and she had to jump to save her shoe. 'Have you no shame? Do you think I don't know what you're at, trying to make little of me and all I stand for? What would people say if a daughter of Ned Flavin high-tailed it off to the Yanks?'

'What would I do here?' The girl was shaking.

'You'll get married, like any normal girl.'

'I won't,' Phena moaned

'Come here to me, now.' Flavin spoke more gently to his daughter. 'I have something for you.'

She watched cautiously as he produced the bag. 'Oh, its from Moran's!' she said in surprise. He shook the container as if it was a sack of potatoes and the coat slid out onto a chair. It looked improper against the wooden frame and beneath a baleful picture of the sacred heart. The girl ran towards it, her fingers reaching out to touch it, but she held them back because she had been gutting fish. 'Oh,' she said. 'Oh, the Lord save us, that's lovely. Whose is it?'

'It's for you,' the old man said, and for a moment, when she smiled at him, there was a bond of love between them.

18

'Now, lassie, we've got a man for you to marry. Will you take him?' He was afraid of the emotional moment.

She slowly wiped her hands on an apron and put out a finger to the coat. 'Could I see him?'

'No,' he shook his head. 'There'll be no nonsense. You'll meet him at the altar.'

She sat down on the chair beside the coat. Her hand went furtively into the pocket and she caressed it. 'Where would we live? What would he do to me?'

She knew he would not dream of answering such questions. Already his look had turned to scorn for her foolish talk. She began to cry and the old man laughed delightedly. For her hand, still stained with the blood of herrings, had fastened itself into the softness of the fur, and would not let go.

HAVE YOU HAD A NICE DAY?

Francis King

Francis King was born in Switzerland in 1923 and spent his childhood in India. His years in the British Council took him to Italy, Greece, Egypt, Finland and Japan. In 1963 he resigned to devote himself entirely to writing; he was President of International PEN 1986–89. His most recent fiction was the novella *Secret Lives*. He will shortly publish his autobiography, *Yesterday Came Suddenly*.

'Have You Had A Nice Day?' was first broadcast on Radio 3, read by Deborah Findlay.

HAVE YOU HAD A NICE DAY?

It was the rainy season. Grey-green rods of rain pierced the towering foliage, hammered the deliquescent track over which the ancient Cadillac was slithering and bumping, and made it all but impossible for Clare, hunched forward over the wheel, to see out.

High up here in the mountains, it was also the landslide season. 'Listen!' Ruth exclaimed and, straining to do so, Clare could hear a rumbling, as of a distant earthquake, followed by a crash.

It was crazy to attempt such a journey. Clare had already told Ruth that twice already, and so checked herself from telling her it again. Ruth would often remark 'I hate complainers.' Sometimes she would add: 'That's what I like about you. You never complain. So many Brits never stop complaining.' Ruth was Australian, married to a professor at the same university in Kobe at which Clare taught. The black eyepatch over one eye gave her square, seamed, jowly face a piratical look. The empty socket covered by the eyepatch was the reason why Clare, not she, was driving. The Cadillac belonged to Ruth's husband, whom she tended to refer to as 'the *sensei*'. Because 'the *sensei*' was suffering from shingles, Clare had been persuaded to drive Ruth to the Naked Festival in a car far larger and far more powerful than she had ever driven before.

Ruth was writing a book about Japanese Festivals. Neglecting his students and his book, already years in gestation, on Lafcadio Hearn's Japanese years, Ruth's grey and patient husband drove her to innumerable festivals. No doubt it was only through illness that he could escape from the dictates of his wife's relentless will. Now it was Clare who had to submit to those dictates.

'Shit!' Ruth suddenly exclaimed. 'What's going on?'

Only a few minutes before, Clare had remarked: 'Everyone is constantly telling one that Japan is overpopulated, and yet we must have driven for at least half an hour without seeing a house or even a single person.' Now, ahead and below, where the road precipitously dipped, there snaked a queue of trucks, with countless people, looking like insects under their umbrellas, scurrying around them.

'Some sort of hold-up,' Clare said.

'Oh, shit!' Ruth repeated. Hold-ups of any kind drove her to frenzy.

Clare halted the Cadillac at the end of the line of vehicles. 'Ask someone what's going on,' Ruth commanded. But it was hardly necessary to do so. There had been a landslide and, at the bottom of the dip down which they had just jolted, the road had tumbled into a ravine. Ruth reached back for her raincoat and, having jumped out of the car, struggled into it. Clare followed her, opening a waxed paper umbrella given to her by one of her students.

'The road has vanished,' Ruth said.

'They're repairing it.' Another statement of the obvious.

Men in baggy cotton trousers and shirts, soaked with rain, were heaving up huge logs, with sudden, concerted yelps, and then lugging them to the place where instead of the road there was a jagged wound of mud, rocks and serpentine tree-roots.

'Ask them how long it's going to take. We're already behind our schedule.' Ruth often used the word 'schedule', pronouncing it in the American manner. She had a schedule for most things in her life.

Clare, wishing, not for the first time, that she spoke no Japanese, squelched over the mud to someone in a peaked cap who looked like the foreman.

He shrugged; said 'One hour, two hours, maybe three hours'; shrugged again. Then he shouted out something to the gang of men and strode off.

Clare translated for Ruth. Then she said: 'No use in getting wet. We might as well wait in the car.'

'You could first tell them to get a move-on.'

'I don't think there'd be much point in doing that.'

Back in the car, Ruth produced a Hershey bar, broke it in two and gave Clare the smaller half. 'Unless they get a move-on, we'll never make it to that inn before nightfall.'

'Then we'll have to find another inn.'

'If another inn exists . . . Ah, well, it won't be the first time I've bedded down in the Caddy.' Munching at another bite of the chocolate, she went on: 'Isn't it odd that not one of all these men has shown the smallest interest in us?'

'Is it?'

'Well, suppose we had been held up like this in some remote spot in Australia or the States or even in England . . . The only women among a horde of truck-drivers . . . You can bet your bottom dollar that we'd be the centre of attention. There'd be a crowd around the car.'

'That's what I like about Japan.'

It clearly wasn't what Ruth liked about Japan. 'Well, I like to be noticed. I like to feel that I exist.'

One hour passed. A second hour passed. Ruth said: 'You'd better ask that man how much longer we'll have to wait.' The rain had now ceased. Saffron-coloured, the sunshine of early evening filtered down through the branches.

'There's not much point. He probably doesn't know.'

'Oh, go on!'

Clare got out of the car. And as she did so, she saw a young man, in jeans and a shiny black blouson, walking towards her. His close-cropped hair was glittering with rain-drops. He smiled, and in quaintly formal English, said: 'Excuse me, please. You are American lady?'

'English.'

'*So deska*? May I please talk English with you?'

'Well, not really at this moment. I'm going to ask the foreman how much longer we have to wait.'

He drew in his breath with a hiss: 'Long time.' Whether he meant that they'd already waited a long time or that they

25

would still have to wait a long time, wasn't clear. 'Sorry.'

Ruth now clambered out of the car. 'You speak English.'

'A little.'

'How much longer are we going to have to wait here?' She spoke crossly as though the young man were to blame for the landslide and for the delay in erecting the temporary bridge across it.

Again he drew in his breath with a hiss. 'Many men working.'

'Yes, I can see that.'

'You travel far?'

'We're going to the Naked Festival – the *Hadaka Matsuri*,' Clare answered.

Eyebrows raised in his handsome face; the young man looked astonished: 'You are interested in such things?'

'Yes. Aren't you?'

Ruth's question embarrassed him. He giggled, hand to mouth.

'Aren't you?' she repeated.

'Such things are things of past. Old Japan.'

Ruth snorted. She began to give him a lecture, familiar to Clare, about the folly of the Japanese in gradually abandoning their unique way of life for a 'rubbishy' one imported from the West. Clare wondered how much the young man, now looking apprehensive, understood. Probably not much. Certainly not the word 'rubbishy'.

At the end of the lecture, Clare asked how far it was to the small town to which they were travelling.

'Two, three hours,' the man replied. 'Maybe four in this weather.'

'Well, that's nice and precise!' Clare hoped that Ruth's sarcasm was lost on the man. With the Japanese, sarcasm usually was. 'We were recommended this inn – this *ryokan*' Ruth went on, using one of the few Japanese words which she had learned. 'A Japanese colleague of my husband told us about it. Not at all luxurious, of course, but *clean*. We were planning to spend two nights there – tonight and the night of the Festival.'

'Maybe you will only spend tomorrow night there.' The young man laughed. Ruth scowled.

Were there any other, nearer inns? Clare asked. The young man was dubious.

Ruth clambered back into the car, a clear indication that, for her, the conversation was over. Clare and the young man exchanged smiles.

'Which is your truck?'

'Over there.' He indicated a mud-spattered vehicle seemingly without a load. 'I come back from Osaka. I carry wood from here to Osaka, Kyoto, Kobe. My job.' He took a packet of cigarettes out of the breast pocket and held it out to Clare. 'Marlboro' he said. 'American cigarette. Better than Japanese.'

Clare shook her head. 'I don't smoke.'

'I smoke much, too much.'

They continued to talk. 'Excuse me,' he would begin, and then he'd ask her some question about her life or life in general in England.

'You like Japan?'

'Yes, I love it, I fell in love with it the moment I got here.'

He shook his head, frowning, as he drew deeply on yet another cigarette.

Suddenly the foreman was approaching, waving an arm and shouting.

'What is he saying?' The man's accent, so unlike the Kansai accent to which she was accustomed, made it difficult to understand him.

'Bridge is ready. He is asking you to come.'

'Us?'

'He is asking you to come first.'

'But why?'

'You are foreigners. It is polite for you to come first.'

The foreman was gesticulating and shouting again.

Was politeness to foreigners truly the reason? Or did the foreman think that in trying out his makeshift bridge, it was foreign, not Japanese, lives which should be risked?

'Frankly, the thought of driving across those logs terrifies me. I'd rather see someone else do it first.'

'I will drive!'

'You?'

'If you are –' he hesitated for the word she had used – 'if you are *terrified*.'

Ruth opted not to be in the car – 'There's no point in our *all* being killed.' The logic was irrefutable, but Clare didn't think that she too could quit.

The young man frowned in concentration as, on the wrong side of the road, he coaxed the Cadillac past the long line of waiting trucks. The car arrived at the makeshift bridge, stretched like a fragile plaster over the jagged wound of the landslide. The man smiled at Clare in reassurance. Such was her fear, she couldn't smile back. If only they were not in this monster of a car but in something smaller and lighter. She shut her eyes. With a creaking of the logs, the Cadillac bumped across. Every other truck-driver seemed to have gathered round to watch.

When at last they were over, the Japanese turned to her with a smile. 'Easy! No danger!'

Cursing loudly each time that she nearly slipped, Ruth had meanwhile been negotiating the crumbling hillside.

'Why didn't you use the bridge?' Clare asked.

'It might bloody well have collapsed, that's why!'

The young man was looking at his watch. Then, shaking his head: 'Too dangerous to drive to inn in dark. Maybe road has fallen in other place. You sleep my house.'

Ruth didn't in the least care for the suggestion. 'If we press on, I'm sure we can arrive before nightfall.'

But Clare, usually so submissive at each clash with Ruth, held out against her. And there was another reason for her opposition. She was attracted by the young man. She wished to talk more to him. She wished to see his home.

After some argument, Ruth snapped: 'Oh, very well. Have it your own way.'

*

The young man, who was called Masa, lived with his parents in an untidily thatched little house by a brook. At intervals all through the night, Clare was to hear that brook, beyond the paper screens, its low murmur insinuating itself into her dreams.

Masa's mother, so stooped and lined that one might have mistaken her for his grandmother, carried in the simple meal and laid it out on a low table. The two foreigners had been given the main room of the house, clearly seldom used. It was damp, with cobwebs stretching across one corner of a ceiling covered in yellowish-brown stains.

After the woman had bowed her way out, Masa entered. 'Excuse me! May I talk to you while you are eating?'

Ruth gave a deep sigh. 'Why don't you eat with us? Why don't you all eat with us?'

Embarrassed, he gave no reply. He edged round the low lacquer table and lowered himself to the floor. Clare suddenly noticed that he had three books with him: a pocket dictionary, its leaves curling and crumpled as though from constant use; some kind of primer; and what looked like a photograph album. He consulted the dictionary. Then he said, with difficulty: 'Pri-mi-tive.' He looked up and smiled, not at Ruth but at Clare. With more confidence he repeated: 'Primitive.'

'Primitive?'

'Life here. Life in my house. Life in the mountains.'

As they ate, he spoke haltingly, with frequent recourse to the dictionary, not merely of the primitiveness but of the tedium of this life. In California, he had an uncle, well, not really an uncle, a cousin of his mother. The uncle had suffered in the War, he had been interned, his citrus farm had been taken from him. But now he was very rich. Masa wished to go to California to join him. Maybe soon, very soon . . . That was his dream. He would apply for a visa and then . . . He was suddenly eager and hopeful.

He opened the photograph album. This was his uncle. This was his uncle's son and his daughter. Americans! They looked like Americans, didn't they? Here was their house. As she shovelled rice into her mouth with her chop-sticks, Ruth hardly listened or bothered even to glance at the photographs. But it was to Clare that Masa was really trying to convey all this, and she was totally attentive. Over and over that one word recurred: Dream, dream, dream. Her dream, as a student, had always been of Japan. His dream was of the West.

Eventually, the meal long since over, Ruth said: 'Well, I don't know about you, but I'm bushed.' Then she turned to Masa: 'I think that it's time we turned in.'

'Turned in?'

'Slept.'

'Yes, yes . . . But first, first I must show you . . .'

He opened the third of the books he had brought with him. The primer. Clare decided it must date from before the War, so yellow were the pages, so old-fashioned its illustrations and typeface. 'From here I learn my English. This is my – my key. My key to my dream.' He turned the pages over. He laughed. Then he read out: ' "Have you had a nice day, Mrs Jones?" "Thank you, yes, I have had a very nice day. The weather was fine and I had a visit from my daughter, my son-in-law and my two grandchildren." ' He laughed again.

'Perhaps you could bring us the *futon*,' Ruth said sharply. As Masa left the room, she remarked: 'Oh, what a bore! Perhaps we'd have done better to have slept in the Caddy.'

'Well, at least you've had a good meal.'

'Not good. Ample.'

Driving back from the Naked Festival two days later, they passed the little house by the brook. Clare would have liked to stop, to have seen Masa again. But Ruth was anxious that they wouldn't reach Kobe in time for a committee meeting of the local branch of the Japan Animal Welfare Society.

Gazing out through the windscreen at the rods of greyish-green rain once more slanting down through the trees, Clare thought of the Festival. It had seemed incredible that so many young men could crowd into the small temple compound, packing themselves tighter and tighter. Naked flesh on naked flesh. Some had climbed up on to the roof of the temple, to hurtle downwards on to the bodies below. Some were actually walking over their fellows. She seemed once again to hear their mass chanting, like the mating-call of a wild animal in rut. From time to time temple attendants splashed water on to the milling bodies. And then there was the same hiss of shock from those on whom it fell; the same cloud of steam rising from the chaos of jostling, overheated flesh. It had been frightening and exciting. And, yes, primitive.

Suddenly Ruth exclaimed: 'Oh, shit! It's happened again.'

'What's happened?'

'A landslide! Another bloody landslide! Can't you see? And there's no one there. Not a soul. We're well and truly stuck until someone comes along.'

Clare stopped the car. She got out. Afterwards she persuaded herself that she already knew what she would see.

Far off, at the bottom of the ravine, lay the wreck of a mud-spattered truck, with logs scattered, like matches, all around it. Logs had also jammed against tree-trunks as they had tumbled out during the fall. She thought there was a body spreadeagled on some brushwood. There was a cheap suitcase, miraculously unharmed. Beside it was a primer. Suddenly, she heard Masa reading from it:

Have you had a nice day, Mrs Jones?
Thank you, yes, I have had a very nice day.

PASTORAL

David Lodge

David Lodge is the author of nine novels including the award-winning *Changing Places*, *How Far Can You Go?*, *Small World* and *Nice Work* (which he also adapted for BBC Television). His first play 'The Writing Game' has been produced in England and America. David Lodge is Honorary Professor at Birmingham University where he taught English Literature for many years. His latest book is *The Art of Fiction*. He lives in Birmingham.

'Pastoral' was first broadcast on Radio 3, read by Julian Glover.

PASTORAL

Dah *dah* dah, dah *dah* dah, dada dada dada . . .

I never hear the opening strains of the 'Shepherds' Song' from Beethoven's Pastoral Symphony without remembering my scheme to embrace the Virgin Mary. That is to say, Dympna Cassidy, who was impersonating the Virgin Mary at the time. The time was one Christmas in the early 1950s, and the occasion a Nativity play I produced for the Youth Club of Our Lady of Perpetual Succour, in South London. And when I say produced, I mean I wrote the piece, directed it, cast it, acted in it, designed the set for it, and of course chose the music for it. The only thing I didn't do for it was sew the costumes. My loyal mother and resentful sisters were pressed into performing that task.

It must sound as if I was already stagestruck, but in fact I wasn't when I embarked on the project. I was in the sixth form at St Aloysius' Catholic Grammar School, studying English, French, Latin and Economics, and intended to read Law at University, with the ambition of becoming a barrister (an idea implanted by my father, who was a solicitor's chief clerk, and had set his heart on my becoming a star of the legal profession). I never expected to end up as a director of stage musicals anywhere from Scunthorpe to Sydney – mostly touring productions of golden oldies like *Oklahoma*! and *The King and I*. I did direct a new musical in the West End a few years ago, but you probably never heard of it – it folded after three weeks. Still, I have great hopes of my new project, a musical version of *Anthony and Cleopatra* called *Cleo*! I've written the book myself.

But I digress. Back to the Nativity play, *The Story of Christmas*, as it was rather unimaginatively entitled. I wanted to call it *The Fruit of the Womb*, but the parish priest, Father Stanislaus Lynch, wouldn't have it – the first of many battles we had over the play. He said my title was indecent. I pointed out that it was a quotation from the Hail Mary: 'and blessed is the fruit of thy womb, Jesus.' He said that, taken out of context, the words had a different effect. I said: 'What you mean is that *in* context they have no effect at all, because Catholics recite prayers in a mindless drone, without paying any attention to what they're saying. My play is designed to shock them out of their mental torpor, into a new awareness of what Christmas is really about – Incarnation.' I was a fluent and arrogant youth – at least in intellectual debate. In other areas of life, such as girls, I was less assured.

But Father Stan, as we called him, replied: 'That's all very well, but there'll have to be a poster advertising it. I won't have the word "womb" stuck up in my church porch. The Union of Catholic Mothers wouldn't like it.' At home I complained bitterly about this example of philistine ecclesiastical censorship, until one of my sisters said that *Fruit of the Womb* reminded her of 'Fruit of the Loom,' in those days a well-known trade mark for cotton underwear, and I decided to abandon my title without further resistance.

Dah *dah* dah, dah *dah* dah . . . There were other pieces of music in *The Story of Christmas*, played while the scenery was being changed behind the curtain, and setting the mood for the next scene. I chose Gounod's 'Ave Maria' for the Annunciation, a theme from Rimsky-Korsakov's *Scheherazade* for the Three Kings, and the 'Ride of the Valkyries' for the Flight into Egypt. My father had a decent collection of classical music on 78s, and used to let me play them on our radiogram, a walnut-veneered monolith that stood in the bay window of the front parlour. But it's the 'Shepherds' Song,' only the 'Shepherds' Song,' that triggers memories of the play, and of Dympna Cassidy. I chose it, of course, to introduce the scene where the shepherds of Bethlehem come to venerate the infant Jesus, but it spread into other parts of the play in the course of rehearsals.

*

It all started one Sunday evening early in November, at a Youth Club hop. Father Stan and I were sitting on a pair of folding chairs on the edge of the dance floor, if one might so dignify the dusty, splintering floorboards of the parish hall, watching the couples shuffling round to Nat King Cole groaning 'Too Young' from a portable record-player.

I was sitting down because I didn't dance, couldn't dance, pretended I didn't want to dance, though truly it was a reluctance to look silly while learning to dance that made me a wallflower. I attended these events on the pretext of being Secretary of the Youth Club Committee: drawn by a secret need to behold Dympna Cassidy, exquisite torture though it was to watch her swaying in the arms of some other youth. Fortunately most of the boys in the club were as shy as I was, and the girls were compelled much of the time to dance with each other, as Dympna was doing with her friend Pauline that evening to the syrupy strains of 'Too Young'; and even when she had a male partner, Club protocol prohibited close contact between dancing couples. That was why Father Stan was there: to make sure light was always visible between them.

> They say that we are much too young,
> Too young to really be in love . . .

Not that I was in love with Dympna Cassidy. That was the problem.

She was beautiful and buxom, with jade green eyes and copper coloured hair, which, freshly washed for social occasions, surrounded her head in a shimmering haze of natural curls. Her complexion was a glowing, translucent white, like the surface of a fine alabaster statue, and her underlip had a delicious pout. When she smiled two dimples appeared in her cheeks which I associated with her name, her first name. Cassidy was rather lacking in poetic resonance, but Dympna – it was eloquent not only of her dimples, but of her whole person. The syllables had a soft, yielding, pneumatic quality that I imagined her body would possess when clasped in an embrace. And how I longed to embrace it! How I yearned to squeeze that voluptuous form like a cushion against my chest, and press my lips on the pouting perfection of her mouth, in the manner I had observed in a thousand cinematic love scenes. But I didn't love Dympna Cassidy. Nor was I prepared to pretend that I did. And in that time and place the only way you would get to kiss a girl like her was to do one or the other. That is to say, I would have had to declare myself publicly as her steady boy-friend.

And here I have to make a rather shameful confession: I thought I would be lowering myself if I courted Dympna Cassidy. It wasn't simply that she came from the wrong side of the tracks, though she did; her large and slightly raffish family lived in a tenement flat on a council estate, whereas we owned our own home, a dignified Victorian terraced house, with a flight of steps leading up to the front door. It wasn't that she dropped her aitches occasionally, and tended to elide the middle consonant of 'butter' and 'better'. I could have lived with these handicaps if Dympna Cassidy had had some qualities of mind to compare with the attractions of her body. But her mind was conspicuously empty. There was nothing to be found in it except a few popular songs, the names of film stars, fashion notes, and anecdotes about her teachers. She attended a technical school, having failed the 11-plus examination in which I had distinguished myself, and was following what was called a commercial course. She was being trained to be a shorthand typist, though her own inclination was to be a sales assistant in a dress shop. I knew all this because I took the opportunity to chat to her – outside church after Sunday Mass, while clearing up the parish hall after a youth club evening, or during one of the club's occasional rambles through the Kent countryside. I could tell that Dympna was interested in me: intrigued and attracted by the slightly foppish air I cultivated when out of school uniform, my long hair, green corduroy jacket and mustard waistcoat. I was aware that she had attached herself to no other boy, though she had many admirers in the parish. I felt sure that she would reciprocate, if I would only make the first move.

But I hung back. My future was clearly marked out for me, and Dympna Cassidy had no place in it: study, examinations, honours, prizes; years of effort and self-denial ultimately rewarded by a distinguished legal career. Dympna's kind had a totally different attitude to life: leave school as soon as you could, get a job however repetitive and banal, and live for the hours of leisure and recreation, for dancing, shopping, going to the pictures, 'having a good time'. Consuming one's youth in a splurge of thoughtless, superficial pleasure, before relapsing into a dull, domesticated adulthood just like one's parents, struggling to bring up a family on inadequate means. Becoming involved with Dympna would, I was certain, drag me down into that abyss. I swear that I thought one kiss would do it, one kiss and I would be set on a course leading to a premature and imprudent marriage. And marriage would not be kind to Dympna Cassidy. You could see what she would look like in twenty years' time by looking at her mother: a sagging bosom, a waist thickened by childbearing, and hollowed cheeks where the back teeth were missing. Dympna would never again be as beautiful as she was now, so I told myself gloomily, watching her leading Pauline in the foxtrot, chattering away inanely about a pair of shoes that she had seen in a shop window. This topic seemed to engage their interest for the duration of the set; they were still talking about it every time they rotated past me and Father Stan.

'You know Mrs Noonan who teaches in the Infants,' he said suddenly. I admitted that I did: she had taught me ten years earlier. 'And you know she puts on a Nativity Play every Christmas, with the children. Well, she's got to go into hospital next week for an operation, and she'll be on convalescent leave until January. I've been thinking, wouldn't it be a fine thing if the Youth Club took on the job for this year? The Nativity play, I mean. It would be good to have something a little more . . . grown-up, for once. Something the young people of the parish could relate to. D'you think you might be able to organise something, Simon?'

'All right,'

'Well, that's grand,' said Father Stan, somewhat taken aback by the speed of my assent. 'Are you sure you've got time? I know they work you very hard at St Aloysius.'

'I'll manage, Father. Leave it to me.'

'Well, that's very good of you, I'll see if the Catholic Truth Society publish a suitable play. I don't think the one Mrs Noonan uses would be quite the ticket.

'I'll write the play myself.'

As soon as he had mentioned the Nativity Play a tableau had formed in my mind's eye: Dympna Cassidy as Our Lady, stunningly beautiful, her copper filigree hair shining like a halo in the footlights, and myself as St Joseph, supporting her on the road to Bethlehem, my arm round her shoulders, or even her waist. I had found the perfect alibi for getting into close physical contact with Dympna Cassidy without incurring any moral or emotional obligations.

'You'd have to show me the script before it's performed.'

'Just to make sure there's no heresy,' Father Stan exposed his irregular, nicotine-stained teeth in a wolfish grin.

I wrote the play, believe it or not, over two weekends. I didn't bother with auditions, partly because there wasn't time, and partly because nobody would have turned up for them. There was no thespian tradition at the Youth Club of Our Lady of Perpetual Succour. I picked out the likeliest members of the club for my cast and, as we say in the profession, made offers without asking them to read. Naturally I approached Dympna Cassidy first. When I told her I wanted her to play the Virgin Mary she went pink with pleasure, but shook her head and bit her underlip and said that she had never acted in her life. I told her not to worry. I had some experience of acting in school plays, and I would help her. I looked forward to intimate coaching sessions in the front parlour at home, with the radiogram providing some suitable background music. Dah *dah* da, dah *dah* dah . . . Did I already have that piece of music in mind?

I deferred showing Father Stan the script on the grounds

that we were continually revising it in the course of rehearsals. But eventually he got suspicious and borrowed a copy from another member of the cast, and there was the most almighty row. He came round to our house one evening, fortunately when my parents were out, grasping the rolled-up script in his fist like a baton. He waved it furiously in my face. 'What's the meaning of this filth? What do you mean by soiling the spotless purity of our Blessed Mother?'

I knew at once that he was referring to the stage direction at the end of Act I, Sc i: [JOSEPH *and* MARY *embrace*].

Admittedly there wasn't a great deal of Biblical authority for this scene. It was an imaginative attempt to evoke the life of Mary when betrothed to Joseph, and before she had any idea that she was to become the Mother of God. I was aiming at a contemporary style in my play – 'relevance' it would have been called a decade later. No pious platitudes and Biblical archaisms, but colloquial speech and natural behaviour, that modern teenagers could relate to. I imagined Mary as a rather merry, high-spirited, even skittish young girl at this stage of her life, engaged to an older and rather serious man. I wrote a scene in which Mary calls in at Joseph's carpentry shop and tries to persuade him to go for a walk. Joseph refuses, he has a job to finish, and there is a kind of lovers' tiff, which is soon made up. And their reconciliation is sealed with a kiss.

Several members of the cast questioned the propriety of this scene at the first read-through. But I argued that it was natural behaviour between an engaged couple who didn't at that stage know that they were going to bring the Messiah into the world. Dympna herself didn't contribute to this discussion. She kept her eyes down and her lips closed. I think she had a good idea of the real motivation for the scene.

After a couple more read-throughs, I started blocking out the moves, starting from the top, but I found that when I came to the curtain line of Act I, Sc. i –

JOSEPH: Mary, I can never be cross with you for long.
MARY: Nor I with you

41

— my nerve failed me. I simply said; 'Then Joseph and Mary embrace, and the curtain comes down.'

'Aren't you going to rehearse the kiss?' said Magda Vernon, who had volunteered to be Stage Manager. She was an odd girl, tall and skinny, with glasses that kept falling off her snub nose, and spiky black hair that stuck out in all directions, as if she had just got out of bed. She favoured long dark-hued sweaters that she pulled cruelly out of shape, tugging the hem down low over her hips, and stretching the sleeves so that they covered her hands like mittens, as though she were trying to hide herself in the garment. It was rumoured that she had had some kind of nervous breakdown, and tried to run away from home, and that her parents made her join the Youth Club so that she would become more normal. But she didn't seem to enjoy it much. The Nativity Play was the first event that had aroused the slightest flicker of interest in her. She had supported me in the discussion about the propriety of the embrace, for which I was grateful. But now I wished she would not interfere.

'There isn't time to rehearse everything at this stage,' I said. 'Could we move on to Scene Two?' But the next time we ran the first scene, I stopped it again just short of the final kiss.

'Shouldn't you decide what kind of a kiss it's going to be?' Magda insisted. 'I mean, who kisses who? And is it a kiss on the lips or on the cheek?'

'It'd better be on the cheek,' said the boy playing Herod, 'or Father Stan will have a fit.' There was a general titter.

'I really haven't thought about it,' I lied, having thought of little else for days. 'I think we should leave it till we have the costumes.'

Later, when the cast had gone home, and Magda and I were alone, going through a list of props that would be required, she gave me an arch look: 'I don't believe you know how to.'

'How to what?'

'How to kiss a girl. I'll teach you if you like.'

'I can manage perfectly well on my own, thank you,'

But later, walking home in the cold December night, I

rather regretted having turned down the offer, and mentally rehearsed various strategies for reviving it. But the very next day Father Stan exploded, the first scene of my play was scrapped, and I had no further pretext for requesting Magda's tuition.

So I never did get to embrace Dympna Cassidy. I got my arm round her waist on the road to Bethlehem. But she was wearing so many layers of clothing in that scene that it was no great experience. By this time, in any case, I'd rather lost sexual interest in Dympna, and was much more preoccupied with her shortcomings as an actress. The manic, obsessive quest for perfection that possesses those who make plays had me in thrall. Dympna kept forgetting her lines. And when she remembered she delivered them in a flat and barely audible voice. If I criticised her she sulked and said that she'd never asked to be in my stupid play anyway. The only thing to be said for her was that she looked sensational. So what I did was to cut her lines to the bone and make her part consist mostly of silent action with background music. I noticed that she liked the 'Shepherds' Song,' and would hum it to herself when she was in a good mood, so I decided to use it as a kind of leitmotif, whenever Mary appeared. This required some nifty work from Magda in the wings: she had to operate the portable gramophone and act as prompter at the same time, but it proved highly effective. I had stumbled on one of the primary resources of musical theatre: the reprise. No prizes for guessing what the audience was humming as they filed out of the parish hall. Our play was a hit. I walked Magda home afterwards, and we kissed in her front porch until our lips were sore.

Magda became my first girl-friend, until we both went to different universities the following year, and drifted apart. I read law as planned, but spent all my time mucking about in the Drama Society and the Opera Society, scraped a third class degree, and to the great disgust of my father went straight into drama school. Curiously enough, Magda had been bitten by the same bug. She did theatre studies at University, became an ASM at various provincial reps and finally went into television, where she has done rather well as a production manager. We meet occasionally at showbiz occasions, and when we embrace each other, as showbiz people do when they meet, she always teases me by saying, 'Lips or cheek, darling?'

And Dympna? Well, she didn't become a typist or a shop assistant. And she didn't lose her figure or her teeth. Somebody spotted her potential as a photographic model, and she had a very successful run in the late 1950s, appearing on the front covers of several women's magazines, until the Jean Shrimpton look put her out of fashion. According to my mother, she married a rich businessman and retired from modelling. They live in a manor house near Newmarket and own a string of racehorses ... I've been thinking I might write and ask them if they'd like to invest in *Cleo!*

BLAME IT ON THE PILGRIMS

Anne Leaton

Anne Leaton is an American novelist and short story writer who has lived some 20 years abroad. Her last book was *The Magnolia House*, and she is at work on her sixth book, another novel. She now lives in Texas.

'Blame It On The Pilgrims' was first broadcast on Radio 4, read by Liza Ross.

BLAME IT ON THE PILGRIMS

15 October.

Dear Edward,

I can't believe you are not coming for Thanksgiving! This will be the first time you have refused to join us for this awful celebration. You know how I feel: your presence is all that sustains me, as I assist Margery in the preparation of that thirty-pound turkey, each of its legs six inches across, predictably as tough as a gangster's bodyguard. (What compels Margery to buy these extraordinary birds every year escapes me. Is it just the American preference for large and tough, rather than small and tender?)

I think your excuse is lame to the point of contemptible. A broken foot? Damaged, I am told, when your mother's wheelchair passed over it . . . This I don't find hard to believe – but it's clear that age has taken its toll on your mother, who in years past was content to subtly deflate one of your dearly loved balloons. But feet go into casts. Crutches – if necessary – are pressed into use, and life goes on. If, that is, one wishes it to. In this case, you are plainly using a regrettable mishap to beg off an occasion you loathe.

I must point out that I myself would rather be tied in a sack and flung in the river than entertain this assortment of distant kin and scarcely remembered acquaintances who gather to celebrate the first meagre Pilgrim harvest on the cold shores of Massachusetts by gorging themselves into immobility. Gluttony as our tribute to these slender early settlers. Only you, Edward, have in the past lifted me out of bedlam and into sanity. Only you, by your mere presence and the quality of your character and wit, have prevented me striking Margery a fatal, well-earned blow during the festivities. God alone knows what bodies will float to shore in your absence.

Please. Change your mind. Put a fresh bandage on your foot and write and say you will come.

In anxious anticipation,
Miriam

18 October
Dear Edward,

I know you haven't had time to receive, much less answer, my recent letter, but since Margery is already beginning to shatter my nervous system, I felt I must vent or die. You, poor Edward, are the unfortunate recipient as usual, of my steam.

I had hoped that Hallowe'en would occupy my sister's attention for some small period of time: the laying in of chocolates, apples, popcorn, and hard candies. But, no, her energies seem immovably focused on plans for Thanksgiving, these moving almost imperceptibly into preparations for Christmas, so that very nearly two and a half months are given over to celebrations designed to bring the slightly impoverished into the fulfilment of their condition and the mildly depressed into catatonia.

Margery has indifferently stocked the larder with Hallowe'en goodies. Now she is planning the Thanksgiving menu. She has already drawn up the guest list – numbering fifteen at the moment. Our traditional 'groaning board' will surely be brought to its wooden knees. I am no longer allowed any life of my own apart from preparations for this celebratory orgy. Margery found me writing my letter to you three days ago and suggested that I could better spend my time organising the litter and trash to be discarded in the interests of presenting an immaculate face to the hungry Thanksgiving horde.

This way madness lies.

Yours in desperate hope,
Miriam

25 October
Dear Edward,

Why don't you write? Has your broken foot taken a turn for the worse? Have you developed an accessory infection? Has your charming mother run her wheelchair over another of your parts? Or is it that you simply intend to ignore my pleas? This is not the behaviour of an old friend. Indeed, as I said that day in the foyer of the Majestic Theatre the last time we met, a little more than a friend, a little less than a lover. Perhaps it is that grey no man's land you hate? Is that why you've given up the one certain meeting we have each year? Of course, I know how tiresome a time that meeting can be, surrounded as we are by cousins, aunts, great-uncles, people married to these, mere acquaintances of these ... There are, nevertheless, moments in the midst of the turmoil when our eyes can meet over the hillock of turkey, over the Everest of mashed potatoes; when our hands can touch lightly as they pass with serving spoons from the platters of candied sweet potatoes. Moments sweeter for being as rare as kisses and hugs from your ancient mother.

Surely even such an unsatisfactory meeting as this is better than nothing ... Don't you agree?

I beg you to reply.

In extremest anticipation,
Miriam

31 October
Dear Edward,

Finally your letter! I can't tell you with what a surge of blessed relief I picked it out of the pile of supermarket circulars and invitations to acquire cheap life insurance on the hall-table. To be lifted so high, then be so cruelly dashed!

You are out of sorts, you say? The discomfort of your swaddled foot makes you irascible? You insist you would not be fit company for a Thanksgiving feast. Do you imagine that I am the picture of equanimity, that I sail unbuffeted through each day? Some four weeks remain until Thanksgiving, yet every cell in her body is already attuned to the event. She has cleaned every inch and every artefact under this roof. She makes lists which are appendages of other lists. She disappears into shopping malls like some comestible down the long dark throat of a crocodile; she reappears after many hours, looking digested. She spends entire afternoons on the telephone, confirming that some elderly aunt is attending the celebration, with her feeble consort in tow.

In the midst of all this, I cling to the hope of seeing you as I would cling to a life-jacket in the roaring sea. Surely you can see that even out of sorts you are better company than an 85-year-old auntie from Sun City, Arizona!

Please reconsider, as a charitable act.

> Your pathetically,
> Miriam

PS. Today, of course, is Hallowe'en. If your mother can be cajoled down off her broom for a moment, do greet her from me.

5 November

Dear Edward,

I seize a moment to write. I have just finished a letter to Patterson Brothers, the butchers who have for the past ten years provided us with those enormous turkeys Margery adores. Last Thanksgiving, however, Frank Patterson sent us a thirty-pound turkey with not only the standard human-baby-size legs, but with a tiny, undeveloped bosom, and signs of having been frozen somewhere on its journey to our table (Margery insists on a bird so fresh it still has a touch of blood under the wings and an occasional feather). It was my assigned task to write Frank Patterson and threaten him not only with the loss of our considerable holiday business, but with the forfeiture of all those hundreds of pounds of miscellaneous animals the good carnivore Margery buys during the year.

Before writing to threaten Patterson, I was ordered to telephone the greengrocers who provide the exotic salad greens that Margery insists upon – the snow peas, raddichio, Belgian endive – to remind them that pounds of these items, fresh as the morning's sunrise, are expected to be delivered to our doorstep on the Wednesday afternoon preceding Thursday's feast. Along with baskets of green and red apples, pounds of shelled pecans, and numerous stalks of crisp celery for the usual ton of Waldorf salad. Margery, for all her insistence on snow peas, is a staunch traditionalist at heart.

You can see how fascinating my life has become, what variety the day offers me. Margery's motor hums with increased volume each hour; by the eve of Thanksgiving the sound will be deafening. We will not be able to hear the dog asking to go outside.

Why do we subject ourselves to this ordeal every year? I do it because Margery insists. Why does she insist? She either unaccountably likes testing her mettle this way, rather than, say, swimming the English Channel – or else she has endured the Thanksgiving tribulation so long that she cannot imagine what it would be like to eat a peanut butter and jelly sandwich, just the two of us, on the fourth Thursday in November.

The television set has gone to the shop for its annual refurbishment. We cannot afford to have this instrument break down with a host of male figures hovering over, watching the usual series of Thanksgiving football games – or perhaps it is simply *one* interminable game, I've never been sure.

I am, as you see, merely nervously chatting while I await your answer to my last cry for mercy.

> Yours,
> Miriam

10 November
Edward,

Your mother's only connection to you is mayhem – physical or spiritual – by your own admission. Why, then would you, on her behalf, distress an old friend who needs you? Why must you spend Thanksgiving with a woman who only notices you when you are lying under the wheels of her chair?

She is only incidentally your mother. In essence, she is the last of the vampires, drawing out your life's blood and spitting it carelessly over the moon. Do you think this is too extreme of me? I can recall even more odious comparisons you yourself have made, in those few moments you could steal away from her watchful eye to spend with me. Are you going to allow this woman to lead you around by the nose until you are an old man, so frail with disuse that even handholding will be problematic? You notice that I do not say – 'until she dies.' This is because I do not for a moment believe your mother will ever die. God wants no part of her.

She will, suddenly and unpredictably, not allow . . . ? Servants will not do – she must have her wounded son hobble along behind her lethal chair . . . ?

I am too upset to continue.

Miriam

11 November
Edward,

I do *not* take back a single word I said yesterday about your old harpy of a mother! Don't even think of asking me to. Some people are born to be loathed. Loathing her, I simply help fulfil her destiny. I know you feel the same but are afraid to confess it. Is that because you think God will smite you? We do not worship a God who smites plainspeakers, Edward. Although He might have a bruise for the hypocrite. I should add that times have changed, as I'm sure you've noticed. We are now free to dislike – even *intensely* dislike – our parents, siblings, or any other of our kin. The pretence of loving all those our infant eyes fell upon has mostly flown out the window. Some will think this unfortunate. I do not. An awful emotional price is paid in pretending to love someone even a mother would send out to sea in a basket.

You should take these words to heart, Edward. It is not too late to save us both.

Despite all, your friend Miriam

14 November
Edward,

The day draws nearer. Two weeks from today we will welcome, Margery and I, the fifteen souls who will join us in celebrating the persistence of the Pilgrims through the first wicked New England winter and into the bountiful harvest. I keep wondering if I will survive this celebration. I see myself playing with my mashed potatoes and pushing the Waldorf salad into new arrangements on my plate. I see myself opening my mouth to greet some in-law of an auntie – and no sound emerges. I doubt anyone will notice these changes in my usually ebullient personality. Nothing short of a dead Mafia druglord discovered on the back porch would draw their attention away from that behemoth bird, stuffed with everything but the small boys of the neighbourhood. Thanksgiving is not for compassionate social interaction. Eating is the heart of the matter. Maybe it was the same with the Pilgrims. Maybe they just sat down and shovelled in the Indian corn and the winter squashes and all the feathered creatures in Plymouth Colony against the coming, wretched winter intent on adding that extra layer of protective fat. Making idle chit-chat with the other diners, but really it was just the stomachs crying out for the teeth to hurry up.

Margery has had the knives sharpened. We now stand ready to slice, chop, dice, and otherwise dismember with the merest flick of a wrist all manner of vegetables, fruits, nuts, and of course the gargantuan fowl. If only I could so quickly cut away the pain of your absence . . .

But I am too tired to tax you further with your perfidy.
Miriam

20 November
Dearest Edward,

I weep with joy as I write this! Your letter came just minutes ago to tell me you would after all be here for the Great Feast: bandaged, but unbowed. With the keenest pleasure I anticipate what only yesterday I viewed with black melancholy. I feel as though a grey shroud has been lifted from my heart. I even went so far as to embrace Margery on my way to write you these few lines. She was briefly astonished, but is too preoccupied with coming events to spend much time being surprised.

I am truly sorry about your mother. But, really, you know, Edward – trying to run the family dog over with her wheelchair is neither very Christian nor very sporting, since the dog is, in dog years, as old as she and probably less adroit, having only its stubby little paws and no wheels. It seems to me that she got precisely what she deserved. It's sad, of course, for anyone to be lying in hospital with a bandaged head and ringing ears – especially on Thanksgiving. But she should have thought of the possibility of pitching out of her chair before venting her considerable spleen on the poor little Corgi.

But let's not spend any more time talking about unpleasant matters. I just want to savour the thought of seeing you in only eight days! Oh Edward, what a wonderful day we'll have! We'll eat, drink, and be merry . . . We'll hold hands – no one will notice – and plan our escape. And in the midst of our revelries, we'll thank God for all little dogs that yap a lot.

Until the 28th . . .

        Your unabashed, plainspoken Miriam

LA BELLE DAME SANS 'THINGWY'

Liz Lochhead

Liz Lochhead is a poet, performer and playwright. Her poetry collections are *Dreaming of Franken-stein*, *True Confessions* and *Bagpipe Muzack*. Her major play successes include 'Blood and Ice' at the Traverse (1982), 'Dracula' at the Lyceum (1985) and 'Quelques Fleurs' at the Edinburgh Festival (1991). She has written a Film 'Rough Trade' (Scot-tish TV) and is currently working on a commission for the RSC. She lives in Glasgow.

'La Belle Dame Sans "Thingwy"' was first broad-cast on Radio 4, read by Grace Glover.

LA BELLE DAME SANS 'THINGWY'

I never used to like it either. Used to be I really couldn't stomach it. Poetry. Hail to thee blythe whatsit, O! world! O! life! O! time! O! *no*. . . Th' Yassirian came down like a wolf on the fold and his cohorts were gleaming on Dover Beach, Earth hath not anything to show more fair, Earth in short thick pants is breathing. I mean, how could somebody of wrote that? And what is he doing the Great God Pan down in the reeds by the river? Re-diculous.

Whenever Mister Luff would go – Right, 3 A. settle down, put away, come on, put away, your *Merchant of Venices* and take out your *Approach to Poetrys* – there would just be this one gigantic groan. Aw *naw*, an ode or something. The usual. To a skylark, a nightingale, the West Wind, Autumn or a Greek Vase or something. A vase! Please . . . What were these guys on? I fall upon the thorns of life, I bleed . . . I weep, I shriek, I pine, I sigh, I boke boke *boke*. ·

So I will never ever forget the day I met her. La Belle Dame Sans Merci.

See, I thought I was going to die. Really. I mean I know we're all going to go sometime and poor wee smouty Cockney John Keats was just about to snuff it, coughing his guts up in big gobs of blood and phlegm when he wrote it. And likely never so much as a cuddle off that Fanny Hingwy . . . But *really*. Die. *Me*. No longer exist. Oh, me plus the Whole World. Next week was cancelled. Also, to cap it, Karen Thompson had just *hud to*, hadn't she, tell me all about all the rumours about Mister Luff and Aileen Walkinshaw? So I wished I was dead. Or I would've if I hadn't of been really really terrified that the world was about to come to an end. End of story.

And this was the Day of The Poem. It all connects up, I firmly believe that.

See, what was happening was yon Cuba Crisis. OK I know it was near two years ago now and poor President Kennedy himself, it's a sin, got assassinated in Dallas the year after nearly getting the whole world incinerated doing his John Wayne and playing at High Noon with the Russians. This is Karen Thompson's dad's point of view and always was even at the time. I mind that, him thumping the table and saying Jesus Christ the hypocrite's gonny get us all killed and what about the US bases in Turkey? But, I mean, Karen's dad stood for the council as a member of the Communist Party. Course he never got in . . .

Karen says her dad wasn't even sorry when Jackie Kennedy got off the plane with blood all over her pink jacket. And here, when Karen's big sister Yvonne brought a John Fitz-gerald Kennedy dishcloth back from America for her mother last summer when she went to be a Camp Counsellor, her dad went really mental and says her mother wasn't to use it. Karen says her big sister just brung it back for badness. From Boston . . .

So you've got to take yourself back – I don't know if *you* were scared – but back to the time when Kennedy wasn't a dead saint, but cocky, and alive, and grinning, with that dark auburn-red hair springing up out his head and swepp back, with his funny Yank accent with the flat 'aaahs' and his fashionplate wife by his side. Squaring up to the Russians. And the whole world held its breath. Me and Karen were really crapping it.

How it started, mind, was this. After *The Archers* it was announced that President Kennedy was going to address the American Nation at something past twelve midnight, our time. My mother just went 'aw' and put on a tightlipped face, and her and my father looked at each other. I said 'What? What is it?' and she said: 'Likely nothing.' I mean your parents are always trying not to worry you, aren't they? See if you're The Only One, like I am, well it's worse.

If you're worried about something or scared, you don't

want to worry them that you're worried, because they worry about you. So you kid on you're not.

I couldn't sleep. So I went down and listened. My mum and dad were sitting by the wireless waiting, and we heard President Kennedy spelling it all out to the Americans and the Russians. Afterwards my dad explained to me what 'blockade' was, and I could just picture all these big grey warships in the black water with their guns bristling, and these – for some reason I saw them as rusty *red* Russian ships with the hammer and sickle in red-black-and-yellow – these were steaming towards them through *icebergs*, emerald and aquamarine and white as sugar, all dangerous and nine tenths of them beneath the surface. OK. I *know* Cuba's in the *tropics* but what I mean is, the way your imagination pictures things isn't necessarily sensible . . .

Next morning the newspaper headlines all had big black letters and the word CRISIS.

Yet everything was dead normal and you just went to school. On the bus there was this man talking dead loud and saying, 'What this country needs is a war. That's how we'll get full employment and get the country back on its feet.'

The woman he was talking to never said nothing, just chewed on the corner of her pink chiffon head squerr. She had this amazing puffed out hairstyle, all beezje-blonde individual curls, each one French-combed, lacquered and lifted out above the one below, certainly must've involved the agony of sleeping in brush rollers and took at least an hour to do – before going to her work! Imagine going to all that bother when the world was going to end.

But that's the way it was. Normal. The *appearance* of normality. There we are in PT out on that freezing November red-ash field, our legs all rid raw and blue blotches with the cold. You'd think we'd have mutinied, and have refused to waste one of our good last hours playing hockey. That explained a lot to me – about the First World War and the trenches and that. I mean you'd hear how they'd had a truce and played football and swapped cigarettes, our side and the

Germans, on Christmas Day. And you'd think to yourself: why did they not just get together and refuse to leave no man's land and get back into their holes and kill each other? I mean why didn't they say to the officers: listen we've been thinking about this, we've got together and decided its stupid, so NAW, OK?

Because here we wurr, just as bad. *Nobody* wanted to be here except Miss Lawson in her red fleecy lined tracksuit, and Marion MacInnes and Sandra Peden her two resident PT pets, the centre *for*wards of course, squaring up to each other like Krushchev and Kennedy, ground stick, ground stick, ground stick, off . . .

All week it just got scarier and scarier. The panicky heartstop noise of the news-tune and the men reading it looking really grim. I kept thinking about condemned man's breakfasts and wondering when my mother was going to crack and start dishing up steak and strawberries.

> Oh what can ail thee Knight at arms,
> Alone and palely loitering
> The sedge has withered from the lake
> And no birds sing.

This is the poem Mister Luff reads us. Last period in the day, we're in off the hockey field, a quick shower, everybody pretending not to be interested in who's got a bigger bust than them (maybe we're all just going to get nipped in the bud and some of us'll never get the chance to grow busts). We've come streaming along the corridor and bumped into The Boys who've just been let out of football and showers and are damp like us, with their cows' licks trained forward into quiffs and the whole all-shapes-and-sizes, rough-and-smooth, gruff-and-falsetto, acned or immaculate ragbag-that-was-3A are all sat there in their desks for what is mibbe their finale Double English with Mister Luff.

> I met a lady in the meads,
> Full beautiful, a faery's child,

La Belle Dame Sans 'Thingwy'

> Her hair was long, her foot was light,
> And her eyes were wild.

Mister Luff is getting married to Aileen Walkinshaw. It's true. Mrs Walkinshaw is a Spirella corsetière and Karen Thompson's mum goes to her. Mrs Walkinshaw told Karen's mum that it was just going to be a quiet wedding because both Aileen and David (Mister Luff's furst name is David!) – both Aileen and David were modern people and didn't believe in all that fuss.

Karen's mum says reading between the lines it's a shotgun because what other kind of bride gets married in an Olive costume?

I'm numb with misery. Ever since Karen told me this morning it's just like inside my chest there's a big lump. Which makes a change from the terror I've been feeling all week. Because another interesting thing I found out that day – apart from the fact that I Love Poetry – is that you can't actually feel two extreme feelings at once. Looking back you might think you did. But actually what you feel is, for instance, total lumpy misery then for a wee flash you forget the misery and it's total sharp terror.

Aileen Walkinshaw. Of course for months there have been rumours. 'Margaret Devlin saw them hand in hand on Saturday night, going into the Gaumont . . .' And, yes, OK Aileen Walkinshaw has gorgeous hair, a perfect Jackie K. flick-up . . . Aileen Walkinshaw – well when we were in furst year she was only about our age now, and, I hate to admit it, even then, she was like a grown-up woman. Definitely much more gorgeous than anybody in our class . . . Also she was Dead Clever, sung the solo verse at the Choir Concert, plus she even won the hundred metres medal . . .

She was the most popular girl in fifth year. Karen's big sister Yvonne said everybody used to hate Aileen Walkinshaw because she was so popular. What Mrs Walkinshaw said to Karen's mother was: 'Our Aileen's a Good All-Rounder.' Well, honest to God, I never grudged her, but Mister Luff, I *loved* him . . .

Course it was Karen's theory you couldn't be in love at fourteen. She'd read it in a magazine. Shows you how much they know. Because now I was fifteen and I'd kept it up for ages. Completely constant. She said it was only a schoolgirl crush and I was kidding myself that he liked me back because he'd told my mum and dad at parents' night that if I stuck in I was potential University material. One thing I realise now I'm older is you shouldn't try and expect other people to understand about love and how deep you feel because ages ago when we had been reading this magazine where it asked the stars what they would do if the four minute warning went ('go down to the beach at Malibu with my English sheepdog and be at one with the Ocean', that kinna thing) anyway Karen and I asked each other what we would do with our last four minutes and I told her that I would tell Mister Luff that I loved him, and she just snorted and laughed and said: 'Yes, or you could tell Mister Love that you luffed him.'

See, why I loved him, it wasn't his looks it was the way his mind worked. The way we could communicate. He picked really brilliant things to teach us, and sometimes only him and me would *get* certain things, our eyes would meet and we would laugh. He loved my essays, when he would hand them back he'd roll up the jotter, hit me on the head with it, smile at me, say 'Yes, Alison, once again, very refreshing' and dump it on my desk with always a brilliant mark and a red-biro comment like. 'I derived much pleasure from reading this essay.'

And now he was going to marry Aileen Walkinshaw, who left school half way through her fifth year without even sitting her exams. Mrs Walkinshaw told Karen's mum that education was a waste for a girl who'd likely only get married and that Aileen was dying to be earning, and the bank was a good steady job and one you could always go back to. Mister Luff was going to marry a Christmas leaver!

I saw pale kings and princes too,
Pale warriors, death pale were they all.

La Belle Dame Sans 'Thingwy'

They cried 'La Belle Dame sans Merci
Hath thee in thrall!'

  I saw their starved lips in the gloam
With horrid warning gapèd wide,
And I awoke and found me here
On the cold hillside.

It was the most amazing poem I have ever heard. It went right through me, melting away all terror and love in a big shiver. I loved it. And ever since I have been open to poetry, especially Keats and Byron and Burns and Wilfrid Owen and D. H. Lawrence, and Elliot, and Christina Rossetti, and all the old ballads by Anon. Anon. is probably my favourite . . .

Two years later, and I sit here looking down at this exam paper: 'Choose, from among the poems you have studied in your English lessons, one which struck you particularly. Explain *why*, indicating how – by clever use of ideas, images, vivid words, similes, metaphors, symbolism, etc. – the poet has painted a memorable picture.'

Well, quite honestly I don't think I could. So I turn over the paper. I think I better do the Shakespeare . . .

MEN FRIENDS

Angela Huth

Angela Huth is a novelist and short story writer and has also written for radio, the stage and newspapers. *An Invitation to the Married Life*, her novel, is just out in paperback. Her next, *The Landgirls* is published shortly. She lives in Oxford.

'Men Friends' was first broadcast on Radio 4, read by Anna Massey.

MEN FRIENDS

Conrad Fortesque, on his way into the church, trod on a beetle. In the silence of the Norman porch he heard the tiny crackle as it crushed beneath his foot. Looking down, he saw the smashed shell, each fragment shiny as his own highly polished black shoes, linked by a web of blood. Damn, he thought: how Louisa would have hated this – Louisa who would rescue dying flies from summer windowpanes. Conrad felt his throat clench. He coughed. Up until this moment he had been all right, in control. Death of the beetle shattered his calm.

He made his way into the church. He was early. Walking up the path banked with expensive wreaths of flowers at the foot of the yews, he had been pleased to think he was probably the first. He wanted time to himself to think about Louisa. But he was not the first. Half a dozen others were already seated, curious vulture eyes upon him, people behaving as if the gathering was for a party rather than a funeral. Conrad took a service sheet from an usher, chose a seat by a pillar from which he would not quite be able to see the coffin. Louisa Chumleigh, he read: 1 September 1956 – 2 April 1992. Not a long life. The organ began to play a Bach prelude. Conrad closed his eyes.

They first met seven years ago, one of those smudged summer afternoons when the tremor of heat makes everything illusory. He stood on a thyme-planted terrace, leaning over the balustrade to admire the descending shelves of impeccably mowed lawns. Friends had brought him to the house for tea, drinks – he couldn't remember which. He had stood transfixed as he watched Louisa, in the shimmer of heat below him, take the arm of an old man with a stick. She

67

supported him as he stepped from the lawn on to the path. Her solicitousness – she had no idea she was being watched, she later told him – was mirage-clear even from so great a distance. She kept hold of the old man's arm – Jacob, it was, her husband. They walked towards Conrad, joined him on the terrace. As Jacob pointed his stick towards the arboretum, spoke lovingly of trees, Conrad regarded his wife.

They had had five years. Five years of adultery, though Louisa would never use such a word. She had made it easy for him – writing, ringing, taking the initiative to get in touch, so that he was spared taking the risk of contacting her. She never involved him in her deceits. She even managed to make him feel, sometimes, that the woman in his arms was *free*. But that was the one thing she was not, nor ever would be until Jacob died. Until that time, her husband came first. If she did not ring Conrad for a week – and the agony of silent days never lessened – he knew it would be because Jacob had made some demand that she would not dream of refusing, although when she did ring she gave no explanation for her silence. And Conrad knew better than to ask.

Once, they had managed three whole days together. Jacob was on business in America. Louisa took the opportunity to visit relations in Paris. Conrad followed her on the next flight. Louisa saw little of her relations. On a warm spring afternoon in the Bois, Conrad declared his intention to wait for her: to wait until Jacob, thirty years her senior, died. He saw at once his mistake. Louisa, who had been laughing only moments before, retracted from him, though she kept hold of his hand. Conrad, apologising for his clumsiness, felt a lowering of the afternoon. 'Who knows what will happen – then?' Louisa said. 'It's something I can never think about, Jacob's dying.'

Soon she was laughing again. Back in England nothing seemed to have changed. Conrad accustomed himself to the imperfections of loving another man's wife, and privately determined to wait, however many years it might be.

Then, two years ago, there had been such a long silence that he had been forced at last to write. What had happened? Louisa rang at once, her weak voice apologetic. Some wretched bug, she explained. She hadn't wanted to worry him. She had been forced to stay in bed for two weeks.

The bug needed treatment. Radiotherapy. Conrad visited her occasionally when Jacob was away. He observed her thinning, skin gleaming with an incandescent menace. Noticeably more frail each visit, she lay back against a bank of linen pillows in the huge marital bedroom whose windows looked on to the garden. Conrad would look down on the lawns, misted with rain, and see the brilliance of that first summer day. A nurse filtered in and out, filling water jugs, straightening covers.

Conrad brought pansies, and elderberry jelly. She spread it thinly on toast, but could only eat a mouthful to please him. They held hands, talked about the past. But mostly sat in silence watching the rain on vast windowpanes. Sometimes, Louisa felt like being up for a while. Once they walked down to the lake and back, which exhausted her.

Conrad learned of her death in *The Times*. None of their mutual friends knew of their affair so, not surprisingly, offered no condolences. He had written at once to Jacob, who replied by return, a stiff polite letter in an infirm hand, inviting Conrad to the funeral and lunch afterwards at the house.

Now Louisa was dead, Conrad would never marry. She was the only woman in whom he had found all the qualities he had never known he needed. Until he found them in her. He doubted he would ever love anyone else.

The church was filling up: men in black ties, women in dark hats. A large man with extraordinarily wide shoulders sat in front of Conrad, uncomfortable on the narrow bench of the pew, shifting about. Conrad recognised Johnnie Lutchins, a childhood friend. Louisa had sometimes talked about their times together in Cornwall.

Cornwall, Scotland, the south west of Ireland – Johnnie and Louisa had spent many holidays together. Johnnie's widowed mother had been the best friend of Louisa's mother. She and her son spent much of their time with Louisa's family. Johnnie remembered his first sight of Louisa, a skinny angel in filthy dungarees Feeble, he remembered thinking Louisa was, at ten. But within the day he had discovered she was tough and daring as any boy. They climbed trees, sailed in brisk seas – the rougher the better, Louisa used to say. They teased an old donkey, put pretend spiders in the cook's tea – always laughing, always daring the other on to greater mischief. At fifteen, Johnnie kissed Louisa in the greenhouse among unripe tomatoes. Then he couldn't stop kissing her. When he went up to Oxford three years later, she would visit him several times a term. He was the envy of all his friends, and showed off the beautiful creature at every opportunity. After he had graduated, and found a decent job in antiquarian books, he finally declared his love and proposed. But he had been beaten to it by Jacob – Jacob, a man older than Louisa's own father. When Johnnie had recovered from the shock, he had tried to dissuade her from such madness. Then he had turned to teasing: 'I can only conclude you're marrying the old boy for his money and his house.' He had laughed, bitterly. Louisa denied this. Neither Johnnie nor anyone could stop her from becoming Jacob's wife.

Still, as Johnnie soon found to his delight, the marital state made little difference to their friendship. From Jacob, who had known Johnnie since he was a boy – indeed, he was Johnnie's godfather – Johnnie found himself with constant invitations to the house. He was urged to look after Louisa, keep her amused, when Jacob was away on business. Which meant that with a half-clear conscience they could go out together in London. Opportunity was on their side: Johnnie considered himself the luckiest man in the world. He knew Louisa loved him, even if not in quite the same way as he loved her. It was only a matter of waiting . . . Sometimes she had frustrated him by her silences, but he knew they meant she was being dutiful to Jacob, and he had no right to be either impatient or greedy. When she had become ill he had spent hours, days, by her bedside, laughing at the many flowers and cards sent to her by 'admirers' whom, she claimed, she hardly knew. Johnnie believed her.

He saw her on the day before she died – asleep, but holding Jacob's hand. The old man sat with fresh tears replacing dried tears on his cheeks, making no effort to brush them away. But when he rang Johnnie next morning with the news, his voice was firm as usual. He was a dignified old boy. He would have been horrified by Johnnie's uncontrolled weeping.

To deflect his thoughts, Johnnie glanced round the church. Hundreds of pansies were woven into ivy round the pillars, and along ledges where they mixed with the reflections of stained glass windows. Candles burned as if it were Christmas Eve. The pews were full. People were hunting for seats in the side aisles. Many of them resigned themselves to standing. One of those, Johnnie realised, was Bernard Wylie. Johnnie had met him and Louisa one day in Bond Street, very briefly. He had only just caught the name. Later, he remembered to ask Louisa about him. She said Wylie was a solicitor – something to do with her late father's affairs. They had both laughed about the slickness of his coat, with its too-wide velvet collar. Today, Johnnie recognised the coat before the face.

Bernard Wylie wore his favourite coat accompanied by expensive black leather gloves, and a black satin tie lightened with the tiniest white spots which he had judged would not be offensive. He stood clutching his service sheet to steady his hands, staring straight ahead, feeling the uncertainty of his knees.

She had come into his office one November afternoon – some trivial matter to do with her father's estate – wearing a hat of grey fur sparkling with rain. Competely confused by the legal niceties of the matter, she had suddenly said, 'Oh, I give up, Mr Wylie.' 'In that case,' he had replied, 'let's go and have tea while I explain it all to you very slowly.'

So slowly, that their tea (at the Ritz) drifted into champagne, and then dinner. He had driven her back to her flat, come in for a drink, stayed the night. There had been dozens of nights since. Nights and lunches, little notes and presents from her, calls from all parts of the world when she was travelling with Jacob. Then, a year or so before she fell ill, there was the final note. 'I'm awfully sorry, darling B, but we can't go on. I realise now it was all *infatuation* on my part . . . and know it was not real love for you either, but great fun, and thank you.'

For the rest of his life, Bernard would regret not having made his declaration – Christ, he had loved her from the moment she walked into his office. But he had bided by Byron's principle of never telling your love, merely conveying it. Had his conveying been invisible? Too late, he wrote to her: pages of the long contained passion now set free. But she did not reply. The last time he saw her was at a party, laughing in the distance with some unknown man. She had not seen him. Bernard had left at once.

And now instead of Louisa he had a second-best wife at his side who would never know the loving man he once was . . . She nudged him, this loyal, unexciting wife, her sense of occasion offended by the sight of a young man standing not far from them in a dark jacket, grey trousers and no tie. In the unknown youth's eye, Bernard thought he saw reflected the same despair that lodged in his own heart: but it may have been his imagination.

The young man, Felix Brown had cried for many nights. Cold, exhausted, drained, he feared he might faint in the long service, but there were no seats left. He it was who late last night, and at dawn this morning, had transported pansies from the greenhouse to the church, and arranged them on his own. Only three years ago, Lady Endlesham – as he still thought of her, as he would always think of her – had come into that very greenhouse and admired them. Said they were her favourite flowers. They had talked of planting and pruning, and made plans for the south bed. Felix had done his best to conceal the mesmeric effect the shape of her breasts beneath a pink cotton shirt had had upon him. He had told her how happy he was to be working in the garden. He could scarcely believe he had been promoted to being in charge only two years after leaving horticultural college, he said. Lady

Endlesham had smiled, and said they must make more plans. Then he gave her a pot of pansies for her desk.

Some weeks later she came into the tool shed. In the stuffy air that smelt of dry earth Felix was embarrassed by the pungent smell of his own sweat. He could also smell Lady Endlesham's scent, a mixture of fragile flowers. In the shadows it seemed to him she hesitated, planning perhaps to mention some gardening matter. Then she put out her arms, and said, he thought – though he could never be quite sure of the exact words – Come here, you handsome boy. Handsome? Gathered to him, Felix could hear the racing heart of his employer's wife. They ran like children through the orchard to a hidden place Felix knew. Lord Endlesham was away, she assured him, but not in a rejoicing way. She sounded almost lonely. Felix was twenty-one at the time.

Since then they'd made love in every corner of the garden, and in, winter, in the hayloft. Felix would marvel how one moment his mistress (as he liked to think of her) was laughing in his arms covered in grass or hay, and the next he would see her in the distance walking beside her aged husband, immaculate, admiring the flowerbeds whose geography she and Felix had discussed between a thousand kisses.

When she was ill, no longer able to come downstairs, he sent up a new bowl of flowers to her room each day. The last time he saw her she was standing at her bedroom window – looking for him, perhaps. He was raking the terrace. He glanced up. Saw her wave. Then she disappeared. And with a crescendo in the organ music Felix knew at last she was gone. Never coming back to their garden. Through blurred eyes he watched the shuffling procession of coffin bearers hesitate up the aisle, and caught the eye of his employer, Sir Jacob, seventy-two at Christmas. He was a good man to work for. Felix respected the old codger, but wondered if he could bear to continue the job now the inspiration of the garden no longer existed.

Sir Jacob, seeing young Felix, the first face to come clearly into focus, gave the briefest nod to acknowledge that his floral work in the church was appreciated. Louisa would have been amazed. She loved decorating the church. She and Felix, before the illness, had done a grand job always at Christmas and Harvest Festival. She had been wonderful with the boy. In her usual generous way she had inspired the young gardener, encouraged him, suggested his promotion – typical of her, always seeing the best in people, bringing out their qualities.

Sir Jacob trod very slowly, in time to the gentle music. In front of him on the coffin lay a single gardenia. He had chosen it with Felix – the best in the greenhouse. Inside, placed in the stiff hands, was the equally stiff card with its private message of love which would fade long after the body had perished.

Beside Sir Jacob walked Louisa's mother, a bent old lady with a still beautiful profile that had been inherited by her daughter. It occurred to Sir Jacob, as he put a finger on the knife-edge of his collar that cut into his neck, that they might look more like man and wife than he and Louisa ever did . . . Louisa could have been his grand-daughter. Walking down this same aisle, their wedding day – but he hadn't cared then, or ever, what people thought. All that mattered to him was their mutual, perfect love for each other. Which turned out to be proven. While Sir Jacob recoiled at the thought of his own smugness, he couldn't help reflecting that never once in their sixteen years of marriage had Louisa ever let him down, disappointed him, betrayed him. He knew he came first in her life, just as she did in his.

The coffin bearers reached the altar, placed it on its plinth. Sir Jacob and his mother-in-law took their places in the front pew. A shaft of sun, at that moment, pierced the roseate glass of the window above the altar. Sir Jacob remembered Louisa remarking on the strength of its colour – 'a small pink pool on the altar steps – did you notice?' In truth he had never noticed, in all the Sundays he had been coming to this church, until Louisa had pointed it out to him. She had opened his eyes to the extraordinary qualities of the ordinary, and made him the happiest of men.

*

The vicar clasped his hands. In the moment's silence before the first prayer, Sir Jacob looked round at the congregation – so many people who would always remember his wife. It occurred to him there was a large proportion of men. Men of all ages, he saw, all with that sternness of eye that strong men employ to conceal grief. He knew some of them: others were unfamiliar. Louisa: untouchable to all but me, he used to say. And she, kneeling on the library floor beside him, would laugh her thrilling laugh in agreement. How proud of her he was. There was nothing like having a wife who was desired by all, but faithful only to the man she loved, her husband.

A MINE OF SERPENTS

Shena Mackay

Shena Mackay was born in Edinburgh. She has published seven novels, the latest being *Dunedin*, and two collections of short stories. She is currently working on a third collection to be published later in 1993. She has three daughters and lives in London.

'A Mine of Serpents' was first broadcast on Radio 4, read by Stephen Moore.

A MINE OF SERPENTS

Gerald found two burnt-out rockets in the front garden when he went to check that the dustmen had replaced the lids properly. Bonfire night went on for weeks nowadays it seemed, with bangs like gunshots ricocheting off the pavements and fracturing the sky. Some of them probably were gunshots. Two of his tenants, Kathy and her little boy Stefan, came down the steps, going to school.

'Got all your fireworks for tonight, then?' Gerald accosted the boy, 'All your bangers and rockets, eh?'

'No, they're too dangerous. We're going to the organised display at Crystal Palace.'

'Too dangerous?! Organised display?! We used to *burn down* Crystal Palace every Guy Fawkes when *I* was a nipper!' Gerald was gratified by the kid's doubtful look at his mother.

'No, of course not,' she snapped. 'Mr Creedy was teasing you.'

'Why?' he heard as Stefan trotted along, skinny as a sparkler with his little plastic lunchbox, the wind billowing out his pink and green jacket like a spinnaker, or an air balloon that might take flight and drift over the rooftops. No such luck.

'Catherine wheels' he shouted after them. 'Named for your mum. Saint Catherine!'

Kathy, with a K, hunched her shoulders in her thin jacket. Pleased with the history lessons he had given the child, Gerald disinfected the bins. His description of his young self as a nipper was apt: he and his twin Harold had been nippy as corgis, in their hand-knit cardigans; biting the legs of other children, up to sly dodges, smirking, ears pricked,

Brylcreemed quiffs a-quiver as the cane swished innocent flinching flesh. The Creedy twins were not popular but their dyadic aspect gave them status. Two-faced, double-dealing, duplicitous, two peas in a pod, they needed no one else. Maggoty peas, some said.

Now Gerald uprooted a painful thought of Harold, with a green weed that had dared to survive the first frosts and flaunt itself from the drain. Harold, estranged and sulking, six doors away. No weeds were permitted on board *Bromley Villa*; Gerald ran a tight ship; if he didn't care for the cut of your jib ... similarly, all was shipshape and Bristol fashion at Bickley, Harold's trim craft. The nautical analogies stop here; the twins had been drummed out of the Second South Norwood Sea Scouts, dismissed the Service with dishonour after several shipmates had walked the plank off the coast of Bognor. Gerald's enquiry of little Stefan about fireworks had been routine malice: not so much as a damp squib would be allowed to violate the back lawn of Bromley, or, God forbid, fire flicker anywhere near the garden shed.

On his way upstairs, Gerald passed the half-open door of Madame Alphonsine and glimpsed her laying out the Tarot. She waved a card in greeting: the Hanged Man as usual, he supposed. What a disaster her tenancy was, and yet he had been powerless to prevent it, putty, or molten wax, in her pudgy, baubled hand. One day a leaflet had come through his door, advising of her psychic expertise in palmistry and with the crystal ball, giving, unaccountably, his address. The next day she had materialised and somehow become ensconced, with her scented candles and other noxious para-phernalia, in the vacant room which he had not yet adver-tised. And since then loonies had trooped in to have their gullible palms read and cross hers with silver, in addition to the folding money she charged for solving Problems of Love, Health and Finance, and casting out Evil Spirits. One con-fused supplicant had brought a sickly potted palm.

Gerald had sought the help of the Church to cast Madame Alphonsine out. Father O'Flynn, sitting in the Presbytery sucking broth through a straw, for a parishioner had socked him in the jaw, shook his head sadly. The Reverend Olwyn of Belvedere Road Reformed played him a tape of Doris Day singing 'Que Sera Sera'.

'Ours is a Broad Church, Duckie . . .' she told him, striking a match on her cassock.

'Necessarily' he replied, squeezing past her.

Tony from Some Saints got a promise from Alphonsine to drop in at next Sunday's Wine and Bread do, and some items for the Operation Steeplechaser Car Boot, most of them highly unsuitable. And Mr Dearborn of The True Light Of Beulah embraced her with a hearty 'Praise the Lord! Sister Alphonsine! Long time no see!'

'Yo, Reverend' said Madame Alphonsine.

Gerald had given up.

Madame Alphonsine heard his master-key in the locks of the tenants who were out, and his footsteps going downstairs. She had heard, too, his conversation with Stefan. From her window she watched old Miseryguts pottering about in the garden, shaking his fist at a mocking splash of pink stars against the cold blue sky; set off, no doubt, by some kiddies truanting from school, bless them. He had been like a bear with a sore head since his quarrel with his brother. The needle in the wax noddle was working nicely. She saw him unlock his precious shed and disappear inside.

Not only Harold would be absent tonight; Gerald's two friends would be otherwise engaged. They missed the fireworks every year. By November the fifth they were right down at the bottom of their box, as still and cold to the touch as two abandoned ostrich eggs in a nest of straw. Percy and Bysshe were tortoises. As if they had copies of the Church's Calendar in their shells, they would rise again at Easter, symbolising stones rolled away from the tomb, their dusty carapaces patterned like chocolate Easter eggs.

'Why do you call them Percy and Bysshe?' Gerald lived in hope of being asked.

'Because they're Shelley,' he would reply. The old jokes were the best. His had amused Harold for thirty years. To think they had fallen out at their time of life, and over their birthday cake. Each had accused the other of eating a crystallised violet before the candles had been lit. In fact, Gerald had eaten it, but he was damned if he was going to back down now. And neither, of course, would Harold. Well, let him eat cake until it came out of his silly, pointed ears. No, the ears weren't silly. Gerald rubbed his own; rather unusual design, that was all. Distinguished. Having checked that the tortoises' hibernating box was undisturbed, he locked the shed. Then a piercing pain shot down his leg. He cried out as something sharp stabbed the other leg. It was as if his trousers were peppered with burning shot. He danced from foot to foot, slapping and rubbing at himself. The pains vanished as suddenly as they had attacked, and he was left feeling shaken and foolish, incredulous that his skin was not pitted with tiny wounds.

He sat down in the kitchen, grateful that he could sit down, with a cup of tea and a bag of marshmallows. As he dunked, a little smile played over his lips as the faint pins-and-needles in his legs evoked happier Bonfire Nights of long ago: the time he and Harold had filled that girl's gumboots with Jumping Jacks, and didn't *she* jump, with her wellygogs going off like firecrackers. Actually, they hadn't. That had been a cherished fantasy; even the Creedy twins had not been so stupid and cruel. But he recalled the exhilarating smell of gunpowder in the air; waiting for dad to come home to light the bonfire, rockets in milk bottles, Catherine wheels nailed to the fence; chucking bangers into the fire, cocoa and burning black and cindery roasted spuds, melting marshmallows on sticks, whose bubbles blistered your mouth; the clanging of ambulance bells and fire engines racing along the streets. And the glamour of those firework names: Bengal sparklers, Roman candles, Mount Vesuvius, Silver Rain. The weeks of eyeing them in the corner shop, planning what to get. The thrill of pinching them from under old blind Mrs Hennessey's nose, (the shame of being frogmarched to the police station). But the most prized, the most wonderful of all, had been the Mine of Serpents. Magic and evil. The fat midnight blue cylinder printed with red and yellow waited magnificently until last to explode its writhing gold and crimson snakes into the black sky.

Everything had changed, and for the worse. Homogenised and bland. Only yesterday in the supermarket he had seen hot towels like the kind you got in Indian restaurants; to be microwaved for use at garden barbecues. Lost in reverie, he consumed the pink and white pillows: light the blue touchpaper and retire. Do not hold in the hand. Do not return to a firework once lit. Every year somebody had returned to school scarred; one boy had never returned. He ate until he felt like a bloated cushion, overstuffed with pallid foam rubber. The thought of the glorious time a spark from the Creedy's bonfire had ignited next door's Giant Selection box failed to revive him, and he went to lie down. The pains in his legs started up, his head ached, he had cramps in his arms. If they didn't wear off, he'd have to go to the doctor. If Harold were here, he'd know what to do. He thought about Madame Alphonsine; she had brought trouble on his house. Why had she been guided to Bromley Villa by her crystal ball? He consoled himself with Percy and Bysshe, safe from frost, fire, thieves and predators, snug as two bugs. He wondered miserably if Harold would be eating hot dogs and candyfloss at Crystal Palace, or watching pyrotechnics on the Thames on his black and white telly to the sound of Handel's Firework Music, while Gerald lay dying.

At five o'clock he limped out to the surgery, passing Madame Alphonsine and a client in the hall.

'... a long robe?' the client was saying, 'OK, and what did you say he'd be carrying? A scythe? Right, I'll watch out for him. Thanks, see you, then.'

Green vapour trailed in the sky, a crimson chrysanthemum showered its petals as he hobbled against the tide of people heading for Crystal Palace.

'Ten pence for the Guy?' two children begged him.

'Call that a Guy? You ought to be ashamed of yourselves!' Gerald kicked the black plastic sack that formed its body, bursting the balloon that was an apology for a head, and yelled as a burning needle skewered his foot.

He sat in the waiting room reading a poster: Follow The Firework Code. Keep Pets Indoors. His were. The doctor could find nothing wrong with him.

Gerald was feeling much better when he arrived home . . . But the back door was wide open; he couldn't believe it. There was a fire in the middle of the lawn, Stefan was capering round it with a sparkler, like a demented elf with a fizzing wand; they were all out there, all the tenants. Madame Alphonsine was handing round cocoa. And most terrible, the shed door was swinging open on its hinges. He rushed out. His darlings were gone! Their box was gone. He ran to the fire, to tear it apart with his bare hands.

'Where are they, where are they, what have you done? Murderers! Murderers!' His voice rose in a harsh scream as they held him back.

'Where are who?'

'My tortoises! My boys . . .'

'But you took them yourself! I saw you!' Kathy was shouting, 'In a wheelbarrow!'

Then he saw it all. Only one person would be spiteful enough to take the tortoises . . . Dear old Harold. With the spare key entrusted to him. The tortoises were safe. He looked across the back gardens. Puffs of smoke were coming from the garden of Bickley. Harold sending smoke signals. Signalling triumph.

Ignoring the grinning Guy burning in a suit exactly like his best, Gerald grabbed the heavy blue and red and yellow shawl from Madame Alphonsine's head and flapped it above the flames; signalling a truce under the shooting stars and sea-anemones and serpents that floated in the sky.

RABBITS

Lawrence Scott

Lawrence Scott is from Trinidad and Tobago. He came to England to be a Benedictine monk and after studying philosophy and theology chose to leave the monastery, and now teaches and writes in London. His first novel was *Witchbroom*. His short stories have been widely anthologised and he is the winner of the 1986 Tom-Gallon Award. He is currently working on a new novel.

'Rabbits' was first broadcast on Radio 4, read by Deborah Findlay.

RABBITS

'I can hardly speak about it,' Marie Wainwright said as she held the earpiece of the telephone firmly in her left hand. She leant her elbow on the sill of the demerara window and leaned towards the phone in order to speak, tipping slightly the tall stool on which she was sitting. Near her arm was a half drunk glass of lemonade, sweating. As she listened to her cousin Inez she stared out into the yard. 'Quite,' she said. Her fingers stroked a few strands of stray hair up the nape of her neck and tucked them into her bun.

The hutches which she could see beneath the pushed-out demerara shutters of the sugarcane estate house stood in a line below the kimeet and mango trees. They confronted her with her latest project for saving money: rabbits. They breed so quickly, she thought.

'You had the children with you?' Inez asked.

Marie Wainwright had six children and was at this moment expecting her seventh child. She said she'd gone to Mr Weston's bungalow to ask him to give her and the children a lift into town for the Good Friday service. 'I can hardly talk about it. I've told you everything, I think. Everything, that is, which I dare say.'

She had remembered saying, *'Come back, you'll fall.' Her two children were running ahead of her. They had looked back at her and laughed mischievously. 'Come back, you'll smudge your best white pants, your new dress.' She had watched as their shoes, newly polished by Baboolal the yard-man, scuffed the larger stones on the gravel road up to Mr Weston's bungalow. She had so wanted to be in time for the reading of the Passion. She'd kept seeing them in front of her and seeing her children standing there before them, staring as children do.*

'What a trial for you, my dear, what an ordeal.' Inez pulled her back to the telephone conversation.

'I so wanted to be there in time for the Adoration of the Cross and for Communion.' Marie Wainwright spoke distractedly and remembered Mrs Weston's auburn hair in the afternoon sun against her white English skin as she lay with her arms outstretched like a cross on the cushions beneath the tamarind tree.

'Mr Weston?' Inez enquired.

'I called, but the house was empty.' Marie Wainwright looked about her own empty dining-room. Out of the silence came the metal chink of hoes on the gravel outside. A gang of women from the barracks were weeding the yard.

Then they stopped, and she could see them squatting below the mango tree, taking some shade. One of the women was pregnant. She squatted with her big belly, pushing her skirts down between her legs. Marie Wainwright watched the women from the barracks under the mango tree near the rabbit hutches. They breed so quickly, she thought.

'You see, the children had run into the yard ahead of me. They always loved that big yard with the tamarind tree,' she explained to Inez. Tamarinds were in season. 'When I got to the top of the verandah steps the door was open and I called.'

'The children?' Inez asked.

'The children? Their innocence protected them. They don't talk about it, we don't talk about it. When I came downstairs I called for them, but they did not answer, and then I went looking for them.'

'You mustn't talk about it, Marie. Why don't you meet me at the club tonight. It's library night, you remember?'

'Yes, the club, the library, yes. I will have to get the girl to stay with the children.'

'You must prepare yourself,' Inez continued. 'They are talking about it.'

'At the club. How on earth?'

'It seems that after you and the children had left, a couple

of young overseers turned up with some of the young girls.
You know the type? And now it's all over the company.'

'How dreadful. Poor Mr Weston. I can't help thinking
about him. Imagine a mother doing that. The house was so
empty and they, they under the tamarind tree, all the
cushions.' Marie Wainwright remembered the cushions and
Mrs Weston's auburn hair.

As she spoke she picked off beads of condensation from
the glass of lemonade and then touched her brow with the
tepid moisture.

'Don't, Marie, don't think about it. Put it from your mind.
Those are dreadful people, quite different. It would never
have happened so in our mothers' day.'

As she stared out of the demerara window Marie Wainwright could see Baboolal going to clean out the rabbit
hutches. The women from the barracks had begun again the
rhythmic chink of the hoes on the gravel.

'I will see you at the club at six.'

'Bye.' Marie Wainwright put down the phone.

The house was silent. As she listened it creaked, and she could
hear the wind in the palmiste.

'Madam?'

'Josephine, a nice glass of lemonade. This heat is killing
me.'

'Yes, madam'

'Josephine, a dash of bitters.'

'Yes madam.'

'Those rabbits.' she suddenly remembered. 'Baboolal!' She
leant from the window and shouted into the yard, 'Baboolal!'
The man rose from where he was stooping. He stopped weeding the orange and red zinnias and looked up at her.

'Madam?'

'Baboolal, the rabbits.' And then she remembered that she
had seen him cleaning out the hutches. 'You've fed the
rabbits?'

'Yes, madam.'

The garden behind the rabbit hutches was wild with grass

the people called rabbit meat. The Wainwright children liked to call it that too, and Marie Wainwright herself referred to the grass as rabbit meat. It was precious and she had to see that Baboolal put a stop to the barrack children with their grass knives.

The barracks huddled there, black galvanised one-room shacks, erected along the grass trace beyond the pasture behind the wild garden.

They had started with just two rabbits and now they had quite a number. They bred so quickly.

She made herself comfortable on the couch under the window in the gallery near the pots of angel hair fern. Her knitting was in a sewing-bag on the floor beside her. Yes, she would take it up in a moment, but she just wanted to close her eyes for a few minutes. She moved and made herself more comfortable, cradling her pregnant stomach in her arms.

She tried to remember what she had seen:

'Come here at once.' She had wanted to put her hands over their eyes. The children were standing in front of the couple, who were lying on the cushions, and staring. It was Mrs Weston's freckled back and her auburn hair in the afternoon sun which stung her own eyes. She had noticed the pattern on the cushions, thinking that she had seen the very same gold and brown English country flowers and had thought of getting it for the drawing-room and couch and chairs. 'Let us find Mr Weston, he must be at the back of the house.' She remembered saying that. *The children were rooted and she had found it difficult to turn her eyes away. It seemed like hours, when it must have been only a few seconds, before she dragged the children away, talking to herself and them, and saying 'Excuse me, excuse me,' over and over again. She had wanted to look back in case she had dropped something, all the time keeping the Crucifixion before her eyes.*

All she'd kept seeing was the freckled back of Mrs Weston, her pale English skin in the sun, her auburn hair in the afternoon. It was Mr Poole, wasn't it? She remembered his brown hands. She remembered the shoes and socks on the gravel path beneath the tamarind tree. The socks were navy blue and the shoes brown. *He had turned his face towards her and the children, but he could have been blind because he looked beyond her and the children, rapt.* She remembered now that they had not even moved from that position. She hated to think about it. *The woman's freckled back, the naked toes, the shoes and socks. They had not noticed them, she and her two small children, rooted there under the tamarind tree on a Good Friday afternoon.* Then she remembered the woman's sandal near her ankle.

She had dragged the children away ignoring their questions. 'What is Mrs Weston doing, mummy?' She had put her hand over her daughter's mouth. She did not want what she had seen to reach the light of words. She did not want this to be her daughter's realisation.

'Close your eyes.' She could see the Pieta, the Mother of Sorrows with her dying son draped in her arms, her heart pierced with arrows. 'Offer it up,' she had said to herself.

The zinnias in the naked flower beds, after Baboolal had weeded them, looked ragged in the sun. So little grew in the dry season, so little, close to the ground. But the trees flowered, the blood of the flamboyant, the red of flame and blood.

The rabbits were nibbling the fresh rabbit meat oblivious of the woman's presence. In the last hutch, which she inspected, there were two rabbits, one humped upon the other's back. She stared at them and lost herself in the staring. The pregnant woman rocked back on her heels and rubbed her hands into her hips. She was lost here for a moment which seemed like an eternity. The female rabbit continued to nibble and to twitch its nose, its face a continual movement of pink and white. The male stared ahead, and the movement of that passion was imperceptible, then suddenly the slightest trembling of the small body and hardly an audible squeak. As she continued to stare, the heat made her drowsy and she could feel the sun on her bare shoulders. She could see the freckled back of the English woman's white skin, the rapt face of Mr Poole, his brown fingers in her hair.

'Madam, I finish the cleaning out.' Baboolal stood watching his madam looking at the rabbits humped one upon the other. She did not move. 'Madam, I finish.' She turned and looked through him.

Marie Wainwright rested. On the bedside table were the paraphernalia of her religion: rosary beads, a mother-of-pearl crucifix, a bottle of holy water, another bottle shaped in the image of Our Lady of Lourdes and filled with water from that miraculous shrine. Above her bed was a picture of the Sacred Heart, and behind the frame was a dried palm from the Palm Sunday procession. She had pinned a medal of Saint Gerad Majela, the patron saint of safe pregnancies, to the lapel of her housecoat.

She began the rosary, beginning with the Five Sorrowful Mysteries. 'The first mystery is the Agony in the Garden.' She meditated on the Passion. When she closed her eyes she saw the rabbits humped one upon the other. She saw their soft vacant eyes. 'And lead us not into temptation.' She saw the tamarind tree and the cushions heaped beneath it. 'And now and at the hour of our death.' The freckled back of Mrs Weston's white English skin, her auburn hair. 'The fruit of thy womb.' She saw the rapt face of the overseer.

The rosary beads slipped from her fingers and fell to the pitch pine floor making the sound of beads rattling in a calabash.

As she walked across the golf course and took the path around the tennis courts, she wondered whether Inez would be there, or would she have to speak with the English ladies who sat in groups on the Morris chairs drinking gins. 'My dear Marie, we never see you now.' That would be Blanche Selness whose husband was an engineer and had two blond children. The others would ask about her boys, 'And what are your boys up to now?' And of course she always thought the boys had done something dreadful again.

The younger ones and the more recent arrivals from England would call her Mrs Wainwright. She would smile and walk on. And always there would be the whispers, and once she overheard one of those whispers: 'Thinks she's a duchess.' Poor people, she thought, so little breeding, a new breed coming out after the war.

This evening they would be talking about the Poole and Weston affair and they would know that she knew and that she had seen Mrs Weston without any clothes on below the tamarind tree with the naked Mr Poole. The young overseers and their young girl-friends would have seen her and her children retreating down the gap on Good Friday afternoon.

The English ladies were lying in easy chairs, sipping gins or rum and sodas, which the barman was just then serving on a tray.

Coming in from the darkness she blinked. She had to cross the full width of the ballroom to get to the alcoves where the library-books were kept. She hoped that Inez would be there. She could not see her, just the English ladies laughing and sipping.

'Oh, Marie.' It was Phyllis Mellors. 'My dear, how marvellous to see you at the club!' Marie Wainwright smiled.

'You must come and sit down with us, Marie.' They pronounced her name as if it were English and not French, so that it sounded like Murray. It wasn't she that they were calling, Marie Wainwright thought, as she retreated from the Morris chairs, seeing Inez out of the corner of her eye.

They would want to talk about Mrs Weston and question her. The baby moved inside of her and she put her hand on her stomach discreetly. 'I must just get some books.' This completed her retreat. She addressed this to the group of ladies in the easy chairs, but to no one in particular. When she turned her back she could feel their eyes. Then she heard the high-pitched English voice, like a dart in her back. They were not whispering. They were giggling, 'Some people are always pregnant, they breed just like rabbits.' Marie Wainwright turned and hurried to the ladies' room. Bending over the white Armitage basin, she vomited, feeling her child heave inside of her.

She sat thinking only of her baby, sweating and feeling

faint. She took a small bottle of eau-de-Cologne from her handbag and inhaled deeply from the unstoppered bottle.

Outside the window in the darkness she could hear the caddies, the Indian boys from the barracks, laughing. She believed they were laughing at her.

CRYING, TALKING, SLEEPING, WALKING

Greg Snow

Greg Snow has written plays and short stories for BBC Radio. His first novel was called *Surface Tension* and he is now at work on a second.

'Crying, Talking, Sleeping, Walking' was first broadcast on Radio 4, read by Haydn Gwynne.

CRYING, TALKING,
SLEEPING, WALKING

'Mummy,' said Grace 'what do babies eat?'

'It depends,' Victoria replied, hoping to evade a long discussion on infant nutrition at seven-thirty on Boxing Day
evening. She was preparing yet another twelve-course snack
for her husband's family and her daughter's earnest question,
while not without its sweet aspect, was a bridge roll too
far.

'What does it depend on?'

'Oh, Grace . . . lots of things. I'll tell you tomorrow. Why
hasn't daddy put you to bed?'

'He's asleep.'

Mm, thought Victoria. I bet he'll wake up at the smell of
approaching vol-au-vent.

'Please, mummy, tell me now. My baby's ever so hungry.
Listen – he's crying really loud.'

Victoria listened to the doll. It *was* really loud, and amaz-
ingly realistic. Annoyingly realistic, in fact. Victoria wondered whether any seven year old mothers had been driven
to abuse their tireless electronic babes. The phrase Assault
and Battery Not Included suddenly occurred to her.

'Can't you go up to your room and turn it, down, darling?
The batteries'll go flat.'

Grace gave her patient-yet-irked look.

'That's what I'm *saying*. I can't turn him down. He's a *real*
baby.'

Victoria felt suddenly cruel at pouring cold water on her
daughter's fantasy. She wiped her hands and went to the
fridge for milk.

'Warm milk, that's what he needs. Have you got his bottle?'

'I'll go and get it.'

'Go on, then. I'll warm this in the microwave.'

While Grace was upstairs Victoria wondered again how her daughter could be so obsessed with babies. It wasn't as though she'd received any special encouragement: the opposite, in fact. The last thing Victoria wanted for her was a life of child rearing. Science; the Law; even Management Consultancy – anything to avoid what Victoria and her friends called Sharonsville. But there it was. At seven, Grace was showing no interest at all in engineering, though she could change a nappy (a *terry towelling* nappy, ye gods) with one pudgy hand. Victoria comforted herself with fantasies of future greatness in obstetric consultancy.

'Here it is, mummy,' said Grace as she appeared with the doll's bottle. 'Do you think it's got germs in?'

'Ooh, I don't suppose so,' said Victoria, unable to stop herself smiling. The microwave pinged and she filled the tiny bottle. Grace watched intently.

'Mummy, if he cries in the night-time, can I come down and warm up some milk?'

'No, Grace. You're not to touch the microwave.'

'Granny let me yesterday.'

'Did she?'

'Yes. Her tea got cold.'

'Well,' sighed Victoria, mentally calculating the hours left before her in-laws would be gone 'I don't want you doing it in the middle of the night, and that's final.'

'He'll cry and cry,' said Grace knowledgeably, as she trotted off with the bottle.

In the absence of a free hand Victoria banged the drawing-room door open with her backside. It made a satisfying connection with her father-in-law's head but he didn't stir. What was it, she wondered, with her husband's family and sleep?

What talent they had, all of them. The Osmonds of snooze. The von Trapps of the extended lie-in. Victoria crashed the tray down on a coffee-table. Her mother-in-law yawned.

'Oh – Vicky. Do you need a hand?'

'No, Estelle, I need five.'

'Those vol-au-vents smell good. Marks and Sparks?'

'I made them.'

'Clever *thing*. Mmm, my mouth's watering.'

Probably the excess from your brain, thought Victoria, handing her a plate and napkin.

'Vicky,' said Estelle, as she shovelled Parma ham onto her plate. 'Can I say something?'

'Of course,' said Victoria, knowing she was about to be treated to another dose of unwelcome frankness.

'Well . . . you are silly, you know – not buying dollies for Gracie. Little girls can't help loving them. It's their hormones.'

'She doesn't have hormones, Estelle. She has Jason Donovan.'

'Well, instinct then. You might *want* her to be a lorry driver, but there's no law to say she can't be a mother as well.'

Victoria felt her anger rise. 'I don't think she's exactly hard done by on the doll front, is she? She got *six* yesterday. And while we're being frank, Estelle, Grace was saying you let her use the . . .'

'Yes?'

'Oh, nothing. Would you like a gherkin?'

Estelle refused a gherkin on the grounds of potential flatulence, and Victoria was suddenly bereft of conversation. There was so little between her and her mother-in-law, and good manners just didn't stretch to forty-eight hours. Grace saved the moment by running into the room, howling.

'Mummy, mummee! Quick, quick – he's been sick!'

'Who's been sick, Gracie?' asked Estelle.

'My baby! Oh, quick!'

For a moment Victoria considered being angry with her daughter. This had gone too far, even for a militant membei of the Keep the Family Sacred campaign. But Estelle was already halfway up the stairs with Grace, and the men had now, as predicted, been awoken by their stomachs.

'Blimey,' said Roger, her husband 'is that the time? We're missing the movie. Ooh, food. Did I hear Grace crying?'

'Yes, that is the time. No, we're not missing the film: I switched the video on. And yes, that was Grace crying.'

'All right, no need to snap. Why's Grace crying?'

Victoria was about to snap again, but she was cut short by two long screams from Estelle, followed by a thump as she hit the floor.

They were upstairs in three bounds. Estelle lay on her back, pale but alive; Grace looked terrified and old; and between them, on the carpet, crying and covered with very real sick, was a very real baby.

Of all the possible explanations suggested in the next few hours, nobody paid any attention to Grace's. Her simple insistence was that she had put all her new dolls in the washing machine and got a real baby at the end of the spin cycle. Victoria finally slapped her, which had produced nothing but silent tears.

Everybody's first instinct had been to call the police. But Victoria could see that Grace wouldn't be up to any more questions, so they decided to wait until morning. Nobody slept. Apart from the mystery of the baby there was the reality of him. He was about three months old and, it seemed, Swedishly healthy. He had bright blond hair, lightning-blue eyes and a pair of lungs with the power to uproot trees. He seemed happy but noisy. All the time he yelled the smile never left his lips. The only worry was that he refused to eat.

Every radio and television news report had been listened to with wartime scrupulousness. At midnight the local pirate station, Bonk FM, said a baby was missing. Roger, inexplicably, rushed to get a pen and paper. Two minutes later the deejay informed a waiting Peckham that the child had been located in its own home, concealed beneath a pile of Christmas wrapping paper.

'I don't know,' said Estelle 'these council mothers. How can anyone lose a baby in her own home?'

'Bloody sight less peculiar than finding one,' said her husband. And that was his sole contribution to the crisis.

By 3 a.m., despite earlier avowals, people were flagging. Little Sven, as Roger had named him, was quiet – though not asleep – and his novelty had worn off for Estelle and her husband. Estelle was making such show of her fatigue that Victoria had no choice but to suggest she went to bed.

'Oh, I couldn't, I couldn't.' yawned her mother-in-law martyredly.

'Please, there's no point in all of us sitting here.'

Estelle made faces to indicate raging internal debate; then, in a tone suitable for one about to lay down her life she said,

'Yes . . . it's probably best. I won't be any help in the morning if I'm tired.'

Victoria resisted the obvious reply, and even managed to return Estelle's dry goodnight kiss on the forehead. She was drained and worried and no longer felt irritated by her mother-in-law. As she watched the older woman's puffing descent up the north face of the stairs she almost felt tender towards her.

When the in-laws had gone a silence developed between Victoria and Roger. On her part it was simple exhaustion. The mystery of the baby, coming on top of the hard labour of Christmas, had sapped all her energy. But she knew that Roger was winding himself up to say something difficult. Eventually he did.

'You don't like my mum and dad, do you?'

'Oh, Rog. Not now.'

'Why not now? We never talk about anything important.'

'Because I'm shattered. I just want to get through tonight, make sure this baby's all right, then take him back wherever he came from.'

'He looks all right. He looks more all right than the rest of us.'

'But he won't eat anything.'

'You never know — maybe Grace was telling the truth. Maybe she did get him out of the washing machine.'

Victoria started to make a sharp reply, but checked herself. Roger was trying to lighten the mood. It was one of his best qualities. One of the points Victoria had given a gold star when they first met. She herself seemed to lack the machinery for being flippant. It wasn't that she lacked a sense of humour, but it lived in a compartment labelled 'Light-hearted Situations.'

Little Sven had been quiet for some time. His eyes remained wide open, his smile as fixed as ever. Even Victoria wondered if Grace's explanation might be true.

'He is the strangest baby.'

'To be honest he's giving me the creeps,' said Roger. 'I can see why his parents didn't like him.'

'I wonder why they picked our house? Do you think they know us?'

'Probably. I reckon it was someone from Grace's school.'

'But what did they think we were going to do? We couldn't just keep him, even if we wanted to.'

'I wouldn't mind, though,' said Roger.

'You just said he's giving you the creeps.'

'No, I don't mean him. I mean a baby.'

Victoria pulled her cardigan around her breasts. Roger really was in the mood for serious discussions.

'Are you going to change the subject again?' he asked.

'You know how I feel about another baby, Rog. I want to get back to work full-time.'

'But you are working. You work more now than you ever did.'

Roger was right. Before Grace arrived Victoria had written for the arts pages of a national paper. Now she freelanced she found her particular line in theatre reviewing could be adapted to suit many publications. She even worked for two rival magazines under different names.

'But I miss going into work,' said Victoria. 'I miss *people*.' Usually when she said this it was enough to stop Roger pressing his point. Now she could see it wasn't going to work.

'If you missed them that much you'd've gone back. We could've got a nanny for Grace. God, *I* even offered to stay at home.'

True. Victoria had chosen not to believe it, but she'd never put it to the test. She turned away from her husband and picked up the baby. She touched his strange yellow hair and he closed his eyes for the first time.

'The truth is, I'm just not a natural mother,' Roger laughed at the contradiction between Victoria's words and her actions. She saw it too, and when she felt his hand on her waist she turned and kissed him.

Grace had had great difficulty getting down the stairs without them creaking. Eventually she'd hit on the bright idea of sliding down the bannisters, which had more or less worked, except when she'd hit the bottom. Now she crept into the drawing-room. It was five in the morning.

Her parents had fallen asleep in front of the fire. Grace knew in her own way that something good had happened between them, for they were wrapped up together and smelled very comfortable. Scared as she was of waking them she still felt compelled to kiss their cheeks. Then she went to the sofa and picked up the baby.

Luckily the washing-machine and drier had a room of their own, at the very back of the house. Grace knew nobody would hear – any more than they had the night before, when she'd put all her dolls in the washer. To her own open imagination it hadn't been *all* that strange when a real baby emerged, though she'd known well enough that the grown-ups wouldn't feel the same.

Grace pondered the difficulty of communicating with grown-ups as she poured detergent expertly into the dispenser. Take Christmas presents. If you told them just what you wanted they ignored you, or said silly things like 'Little girls who ask don't get'. The dolls were a good example. Grace never had asked for dolls, not from anybody. She'd asked for a *baby*. But when ever she did, her mother always

103

made her put the knives and forks out for dinner, or told her to get ready for bed. And now, finally, when God or someone had given her a baby brother she was being forced to put him back in the washing machine.

He went in without a sound, as she knew he would. She kissed him goodbye with the name she'd given him. Jason. Then she sat down to watch the drum turn back and forth and wait for her six silly dolls to reappear. At least they'll be clean, she thought, as the comforting rhythm of the machine sent her to sleep.

In the drawing-room Victoria and Roger curled closer. Grace's wish was already granted in her mother, though there was little chance of his being named Jason.

LEAVING DOYLE'S CROSS

Frank Ronan

Frank Ronan was born in Co. Wexford, has lived in London and Scotland and is now based in Dublin and Normandy. His three novels are *The Men Who Loved Evelyn Cotton* which won the *Irish Times* Aer Lingus Irish Literary Prize; *A Picnic in Eden* and *The Better Angel*. He is now working on a fourth novel.

'Leaving Doyle's Cross' was first broadcast on Radio 4, read by Sorcha Cusack.

LEAVING DOYLE'S CROSS

For a great part of the journey out from Doyle's Cross to Peshawar, Eileen Patterson-Smythe (Cullen that was) was preoccupied with expectation. In 1936 you did not travel from County Wexford to the foothills of the Himalayas for trivial or whimsical reasons: nothing short of a whole change of life could justify the days of packing her trousseau under her mother's vicious eyes, the embarrassment of her father's whiskey tears at parting, the squalor of the packet to England, and a week of playing the poor relation to her new in-laws at Salisbury. And what right had they to take such airs and mock her accent behind her back? She should have realised it was only sour grapes that made these hens look down their narrow English noses at her. She had married, had stolen, their brother; the only son and heir. Had deprived them of the sole male, the youngest member of their family, and for this castration they were paying her back in drops of venom.

'Good heavens Eileen. What have you been doing with Charles? He looks dreadful.'

Eileen looked out across the lawn to where Charles was sitting in a deckchair in white clothes and a straw hat, and tried to remember what he had looked like before and which made him seem so dreadful now. She saw what she had always seen: the silhouette of a British Army Officer in mufti. He was doing nothing and appeared to be thinking nothing, and what was more he showed every sign of being contented in that state, or at least of being accustomed to it. Eileen smiled at the Patterson-Smythe sisters, as though this latest barb had been a pleasantry, and tried not to notice the way their eyes were going over her Dublin-made dress. Stitch by stitch.

*

To begin with, the boredom of days at sea was a relief when compared with her stay at Salisbury. But as her own conversation petered out, Charles' natural taciturnity became burdensome. She would begin to tell him things, and halfway through a sentence would remember that it was something she had told him before, and she would stop abruptly. Charles would nod at her in his vacant manner as if she had finished her story, and he would say, 'I say.'

She was beginning to think that 'I say' was her Christian name. He never called her Eileen, or Darling. In revenge, she stopped calling him Charley as she used to, and said 'Charles!' in a tone of voice that one of his sisters might have used. She did it first for a joke. But when he seemed not to notice she kept it up until it was habitual.

'Charles!'

'I say?'

It was sunset on the Mediterranean and she was a new bride, three-and-a-half weeks into her marriage.

'Oh nothing. I was just wondering about India.'

He made a noise of satisfaction in his throat, and for a moment his eyes became less vacant, as though the mention of India had conjured up a pleasant memory – of sticking pigs perhaps or long silent evenings in the company of brother officers.

She shuffled the cards that were in her hand and laid out another row of Patience. The cards had a picture of the Taj Mahal on the back: a present from Caroline O'Grady.

Caroline had been keen on the marriage: 'You're lousy with luck Eileen Cullen. India! I'll be stuck in Doyle's Cross in the rain the rest of my life while you're out there in the hot sun surrounded with jewels and maharajahs and tigers on leads like greyhounds.'

She had difficulty sleeping at sea. The instability of the ship disturbed her dreams and she woke often. More often as they headed south into the heat. When she woke in the undulating dark, she remembered the faces and tones of Charles' sisters at Salisbury. And without knowing why she was doing it, she found herself practising their vowels and consonants aloud, to the accompaniment of Charles' breathing and the hum of the ship's engines far below.

'Strawberries,' she would say. 'Raspberries. *Guzbriz*.'

At Port Said, Charles went ashore for an hour, and she declined to accompany him because of the heat. She regretted her refusal ten minutes after he had gone and walked the decks on the landward side of the ship, watching out for his return. She would have liked to think that this was love but it was not. She walked because it was so hot that when she sat still her back stuck to the deckchair. She looked out for him because in his company she had not made the acquaintance of any of the other passengers. She walked slowly, with her arms held slightly away from her sides to prevent sweat accumulating. 'Strawberries. Raspberries. *Guzbriz*,' she repeated.

'Summer clothes me eye,' she thought as she pulled the damp sleeve of her dress away from her arm. Caroline O'Grady had gone with her to Dublin to help her choose, and everything they had bought was in the lightest material possible. Dresses you would freeze in on a summer's day in Doyle's Cross. Caroline had warned that the heat would be unimaginable. She had read it in a novel. And Port Said was still a long way north of the tropics. Eileen couldn't imagine how she would live in these temperatures without dying. She watched the men who squatted by the quay and allowed flies to roam their bodies. She wondered if it was because they had dark skin and whether dark skin would be less sensitive to the legs of a fly than white skin. She longed to ask someone, but couldn't think of a way to phrase a question which didn't sound mildly obscene. She consoled herself that there would be plenty of people with dark skin in India whom she could ask once she had got to know them.

Strawberries, raspberries, *guzbriz*. Patterson-Smythe, the Colonel's bride. At forty-two, Charles might have been considered a little old for her, but you couldn't have everything;

and Eileen, at twenty-three, was getting to be a bit of an old maid herself. She hadn't fallen in love with him. She had fallen for him on the rebound, because he seemed kind, and harmless, and he had said something which had made her laugh at a time when she thought that she might never laugh again. It was odd, she thought, that this humorous side to him had not been evident since. They had married at the small Protestant church in Doyle's Cross within a month of meeting. The haste was justified because of Charles' need to return to India once his leave was up. There was a garrison, apparently, in need of his command. The Rector, given a choice between a rushed wedding and unwashed hordes rushing over the Khyber Pass, had allowed himself to be swayed in favour of the opinions of Eileen's mother. He may also have taken into account the fact that Mrs Cullen was the sort of woman you didn't cross unless you had set your sights on another, distant, parish.

Eileen walked the deck at Port Said, and mulled over the idea of dinner parties. One of the few things Charles had told her was that, as the Colonel's wife, she would be obliged to give dinner parties. She thought of black bejewelled guests and punkahs causing eddies in the smoke trails from long cigarettes. These were scenes which Caroline O'Grady had described to her when persuading her to accept Charles' proposal. Advantages she could have as Mrs Charles Patterson-Smythe, which would have been unthinkable if she had realised her original plan, and become Mrs Christopher Connors.

She took an extraordinary pleasure in imagining that Christopher Connors would turn up at her dinner table one day, and sit in starvation corner, watching her playing the hostess. Longing and regret palpable on his face.

She tried to think of a sentence with the word *gooseberries* in it so that she might show off her command of Patterson-Smythe-English in front of Christopher.

'*Do* have some more pudding. It is made with fresh *guzbriz*.'

She was then rather alarmed to think that they might not

have fresh gooseberries in India, and she could think of no other shibboleth to equal the fruit.

A voice at her shoulder said, 'I say.' She turned to see Charles, who had come up the gangplank without her noticing.

Although it was even hotter in Bombay than it had been at Port Said, by some physiological quirk she had adjusted to the heat by the time she went ashore, and the train journey to Delhi which might have been unbearable became an adventure of colour and incident. Outside the train window men in pink dhotis tended cows with gilded horns and the earth rose in clouds of red dust in the wake of women swathed in silver thread and blue. And a young subaltern was more than polite to her when Charles had left her alone for ten minutes on the platform at Delhi. When he removed his cap to her he had muscles which rippled across his forehead, which was something you noticed because half his forehead was brown and half of it white. The white half was surmounted with brown hair and he gave the impression of a walnut and cream cake she had once had in Waterford.

She moved her left hand slightly, so that the ring showed, and he melted away into the crowd. Other women would get off the train who would be better suited to his approaches.

The succession of trains, and the endless days aboard them lulled her into a state of contentment. Whenever she saw something new out of the window she would point to it and call Charles' name, and he would explain it in two words or less, by naming it and sometimes adding an adjective.

'Sadhu,' he might say. 'Rum-chaps.'

By cobbling together his explanations with what she remembered of Caroline O'Grady's fictions, Eileen began to form an idea of the country she was to live in. It wasn't until they had reached a point halfway between Lahore and Rawalpindi that something in the atmosphere made her feel uneasy. It was something so unexpected that at first she wouldn't express her sensation of it for fear that she might have imagined it. It was when her teeth began to chatter that she was compelled to mention it to Charles.

'Why is it cold? Aren't you cold?'

He looked at her somewhat surprised, and nodding in the direction of the window said, 'Himalayas. Freezing.'

They had started out at the end of a European summer and spent much of the autumn travelling through the tropics, and now they were going north into a Himalayan winter. Eileen focused hard out of the window expecting to make out snow-capped mountains in the distance.

'Himalayas!' she said. 'You never mentioned anything about the Himalayas! India. you said.'

She was saved from bursting into tears by the incomprehension on his face:

'I haven't a stitch, I brought all summer clothes. I thought we were going somewhere hot.'

At the mention of women's clothing, Charles became speechless with embarrassment. It wasn't a subject he had been prepared for by bachelor life on the North-East Frontier. He stared at the toecaps of his shoes and waited to see if the problem would solve itself, or whether he would have to think of a solution.

'I wasn't prepared for this,' she said.

'Ah,' He knew the answer to that one: 'Time spent doing a reconnaissance.'

'What?'

'Is never time wasted,'

That was when she burst into tears, and he realised it was up to him to deal with the situation. He ran the words 'Cold' and 'Shock' through his brain until they met with the solution. 'Whiskey.' He pulled a small case down from the overhead rack and extracted a whiskey flask from it and poured some of the liquid into the cap of it.

'This'll warm you up.'

The whiskey proved to be an adequate solution in the short term. But there came a moment when Eileen, although too inebriated to feel the cold to any great extent, was shivering in a rather alarming way. Charles jumped off the train at the next stop and returned in three minutes with a sort of large coat made of goatskin.

'All I could find . . . Warm though.'

He wrapped the coat around her. Tenderly, she thought. He sat back in his seat to admire his handiwork. 'I say,' he said, and she smiled at him. But then he added, 'What a pong.'

It was true that the goatskin had not been cured to perfection but it was warm and Eileen slid into the corner and fell asleep. She was woken by a hand on her shoulder and a voice: 'I say.' She opened her eyes to see Charles beaming down at her.

'We're here,' he said. 'And guess what? They've got the band out.'

Eileen Patterson-Smythe (Cullen that was) staggered off the train reeking of goatskin and whiskey and wearing the coat of an Afghan shepherd. She was still drunk enough not to feel the embarrassment that would creep upon her later at the memory of this moment. On the platform the town and garrison dignitaries stood in rows to have their hands shaken and a full military band played Scotland The Brave to welcome the Colonel's new bride. At her side, supporting her by the elbow, Charles glowed with pleasure at being back among his own kind.

COWBOYS

Stephen Amidon

Stephen Amidon was born in Chicago and educated at Wake Forest University. He is the author of two novels, *Thirst* and *Splitting the Atom* and a book of short stories, *Subdivision*. He is now writing a third novel and living in London with his wife and two children.

'Cowboys' was first broadcast on Radio 4, read by Garrick Hagon.

COWBOYS

I recently went back to Detroit for my parents' fortieth wedding anniversary. It was a surprisingly joyous affair, considering it was held at the local union hall – a place I'd always associated with strikes and unemployment and the funerals of beaten old men. But on that night, my parents seemed happy and in love; a welcome change from the state of conflict that had gripped their marriage for as long as I could remember. I was particularly struck by the way they danced together, with such buoyant skill that you'd have thought they'd danced like this every night for the past forty years. Swept up by the mood of the occasion, I accepted their invitation to stay on for a few days afterwards, even though I was inundated with work back at the office.

The day after the party my dad surprised me by suggesting we go visit his father at the old folks' home where they'd kept him since his second stroke. That had been seven years ago. I'd only seen Grandpa Frank once since then, taking my wife and son for a visit not long after his confinement. It was a disastrous, hellish trip. My son was driven to tears by the grasping hands and plaintive voices that followed him down the halls; my wife almost gagged at a chance sighting of a soiled bedpan. To make matters worse Grandpa Frank failed to respond to us at all. He sat oblivious in his wheelchair, his head bobbing to the incessant rhythms of senility.

Despite that experience, I readily agreed to accompany my dad. It seemed important to him that we go. We didn't say much on the drive out there, both of us tired and a little hung over from the night before. It had begun to snow and the roads were getting slick. When we entered the home I recoiled a bit at that familiar ammonia smell, the hollow echo our shoes made on the polished floor. But none of the old people called out to me as I passed, watching me instead with spooky disinterest. I was glad about this until I figured out that I'd grown too old to remind anybody of their kid.

Strangely enough, Grandpa Frank was sitting in the same place he'd been seven years earlier, directly under the TV in the rec room, facing out, so that you'd have to look at his face if you lowered your eyes from the program you were watching. For a moment I had the absurd idea that he hadn't moved since I last saw him. We scraped some chairs across the floor and took our places in front of him. The TV chattered above us. Somebody winning some money. A nurse was laughing somewhere. I asked my dad what we were supposed to do.

'You can talk to him, you can just sit here, hell, you can play the harmonica if you want,' he said. 'It's no skin off his teeth. I used to think it was helpful talking to him until one day – it was the day after they forced me to retire – I didn't feel much like talking and he didn't seem to mind. So now I usually just sit here for a while, then go grab some lunch.'

I looked at my grandfather. I'd always known him to be a taciturn, vaguely intimidating man, so I'd be lying if I said his senility had robbed the planet of some great light. Still, the opacity of his eyes, the ungrowing stubble on his chin, the chemical blue of his lips – it was a tough sight to stomach. I kept on waiting for him to do something, though I knew the only thing he could do different was die. So I looked at my father instead and told him it must be tough for him.

'Yeah, I guess, though you get used to it. The only thing that bothers me is what he thinks about in there, if he thinks at all. I hope they're good thoughts. I mean, he had some heavy crap fall on him in his day, what with getting wounded in the war and then being called a scab during that strike, even though it was essential maintenance work he was doing. I just hope he has a hold on some of the good stuff to keep him company.'

I asked him like what.

'Well, those years he was a conductor on the Erie and

118

Lackawana Railway, before he got his union card and settled down at General Motors. Those must have been some good years. You know, it was during the Jazz Age, the Roaring Twenties. Good time for trains, they say.'

We both looked at grandpa. He wasn't giving any clues as to what was on his mind.

'Best, though, would be if he still had a hold on that year he was cowboy.'

I looked at Dad. He wouldn't meet my eye. This was news to me, this cowboy thing. I asked him what the hell he was talking about.

'Yeah, I knew that one'd give you a jolt. But it's true. Just before the First World War, he dropped out of high school and went to Montana, where he worked for a year as an honest to God cowboy. He had a hat, lariat, horse – the whole nine yards. There's a photo of him all decked out somewhere back at home. Man, did he used to tell some stories about that. Not lies about gunfights and saloons and all that stuff you see in the movies. But real stories; stories about the work. About the muffled sound a cow makes suffocating after it falls into a ravine hidden by fresh powder. About how good a justborn calf feels in your hands on a cold winters' morning, and some Indian telling him that was a surefire cure for frostbite, though you had to touch the calf the moment it came out. Things like that.'

I looked at my grandfather's placid face and asked what on earth had made him quit.

'War. He'd done it as a lark, you know, and old Black Jack Pershing seemed to have a better lark on offer. And then, after getting that wound and coming home, well, I guess going back seemed out of the question. He once told me that after what he saw that day in Flanders, it seemed like it was time to settle down a bit.'

We sat in silence for a while as a wave of resentment welled in me. I finally asked my father why he hadn't told me this before, this thing that gave the long gone man sitting before us a whole new dimension.

'Yeah, I thought you'd be cheesed off about not knowing

about this, but just hold your water for a second. There was a reason for my keeping it from you, which seemed to make sense at the time. I never told you because of something he said to me once. It was when I was twenty and all packed to head for the coast. He came into my bedroom and stood in the doorway and said, well, I know I can't stop you, but I just wish I hadn't filled your head with all those cowboy stories when you were a young man. Maybe then you wouldn't be doing this fool thing.'

My anger subsided a bit, I recalled how, when he was nineteen, my dad had dropped out of college and headed to Hollywood with ideas of becoming a stuntman. It's funny, when I tell people about this now. They say it sounds romantic, but all the while I was growing up it was seen as a great family sin, referred to in dark tones and whispered asides. In fact, my father used this episode to prod my sister and me into sticking at our studies, chasing me right through law school with the spectre of his indiscretion. Even my mother got in on the act, telling us if we didn't stay in school we might end up like our father, forced to toil for The Man our whole life. For a long time we'd assumed he hadn't worked at all out there, though a raid on his closet when I was in my teens had yielded a yellowed contract for a day's work on a film called *Red Runs the River*. When I was an undergraduate I happened to catch it on TV late one night and saw my dad's brief moment of fame, being beaten to the draw by Randolph Scott or somebody. At the time I figured his shame had something to do with this inglorious image – though now I was beginning to realise there was something other than shame behind his silence.

'You see,' he was saying, 'that's why I never told you about it until now. When you were growing up, especially when you'd go on about your grandfather being such an old stick in the mud, I'd be tempted to say – but he was a cowboy, damnit. But I couldn't tell you. I thought those stories would have planted the same kind of rough and tumble dreams in your head that they did in mine. Make you do the same fool thing when you were a young man that he and I did. And I feared that would mean you'd end up like us, working stiffs with union cards, clocking on and clocking off for hourly wages.'

I asked him to tell me the truth about his year in LA.

'Best damn year of my life, bar none,' he said. 'Oh sure, I was broke and didn't work much, but I had me a whale of a time. One time we went out to Joshua Tree to shoot a scene on this film called *Red Runs the River*, which I'm sure you never heard of. And after we wrapped we threw a dance, right there on the set, and these Mexican girls took a bus up from where they were picking fruit down in the Imperial Valley. Man, the way those girls danced, I'm tellin' you. There was this one, you could smell the fruit on her, the oranges and the lemons . . .'

His eyes grew momentarily distant. I thought about my parents dancing the night before at the union hall, the startling abandon of my father's feet.

'So why are you telling me this now?'

'It's just that sometimes I wonder if I made a mistake, keeping his story from you and then pretending I regretted my little spell of madness. I mean, if I end up like this, like him, at least I know I got that year out on the coast, that dance at Joshua Tree to think about. And he's got Montana. I just wonder what you'll have, and if it's nothing, I wonder if it's my fault, protecting you from something that was your birthright. Look, I know it's a silly thought, because you have so much more than we ever had, what with being a partner in that firm of yours now. Nobody can force you to retire from that until you're good and ready, and that's a fact.'

He paused for a moment.

'Anyway. Just something I wanted you to know before you went home.'

We both looked at Grandpa Frank, locked in his oblivion. I searched for an answer to my father's concern: some words that would assure him that he'd done the right thing. But sitting there, my grandfather before us, almost looking at us, I knew there were no words; I wasn't sure my dad had done the right thing, either.

'Let's go get some lunch,' he said, after a while.

It was no longer snowing when we left. A bright sun had got to work on what had fallen, turning it into a grey mush. We didn't speak about cowboys again that day or any day, talking instead about my job, his retirement, our plans to build an extension on the house so he and mom could visit more often.

I flew back to Baltimore that night – something had come up at work. My grandfather died soon after that but I couldn't go to the funeral, since it would have meant missing my son playing the lead in his school production of *Our Town*. My dad understood, of course. In fact, a few days later that ragged old picture of my grandfather in his cowboy gear arrived in the mail. He looks nothing like you'd expect – no chaps, no lasso, no sidearm. Just pressed blue jeans and an ugly sheepskin coat. His beaten, weathered hat looks like it couldn't hold ten ounces, much less ten gallons. Still, stare at it for a while and you get the point. I had a local photographer touch it up a bit and put a frame around it. Then, when my son was out getting into some trouble or another, I snuck into his room and hung it over his bed.

THE RAILINGS

Ronald Frame

Ronald Frame has written dramas for radio and television and his short stories have been broadcast on Radio 3 and 4. His new book, his eleventh, a novel called *The Broch*, will be published in the summer. He lives in Glasgow.

'The Railings' was first broadcast on Radio 4, read by Nigel Anthony

THE RAILINGS

He'd been expecting to find himself, literally, behind bars. But the building was modern, and remarkably bright, and the only screens were of plate glass. An 'open prison' was a contradiction in terms, but apt: his adult life had been a succession of contradictions, after all.

Instead he dreamed about metal bars when he was in his room, with the door unlocked, his spartan but unprisonlike room. Or, rather, he dreamed about metal railings. The ones they'd always had in front of the house. Absurd things, a screen to protect their privacy from the road. Iron, painted black, each rod tipped with a fleur-de-lys motif. Their end of the town had had aspirations beyond its location, but because he'd lived there since he was two years old and grown up with its values he had failed to observe its pretensions.

Then at a certain point, during the War – a couple of weeks before his seventeenth birthday – the railings in front of the house had been requisitioned for the War effort: melted down to make a tank, or a portion of a gunship, or a fresh supply of rifles. The day they lost the railings was the hottest of the year. The team of workers arrived to do their work, equipped with torches and clamps and saws. A lorryload of men: not Army types, but labourers from the towns, excused service for some reason. They all seemed able-bodied enough. One in particular: just about the same age as himself.

He was studying for his exams that morning, and had been granted a few hours off from the timetable at the grammar school. His bedroom was at the front of the house, the small bedroom above the front door, next to his parents' room with the bay, now his mother's room. His desk was placed directly in front of the window. He was sitting at the desk looking out. The conditions were all wrong for exams. The heat and the War. His father was stationed out on a ship, somewhere about Malta, although it was hush-hush and he wasn't allowed to say, even to them. His mother was worried about that, as she worried about most things. She had been worried about losing the railings too, on to the road, and became more worried when the neighbours told her she could plant a hedge next to the low wall that would be left.

Hedges took a lot of growing, and the house meantime would look bald and – well, more common. Their sandstone house had benefited from the appearance of the railings. They had pulled the terrace up in the world, never mind that the railings had only been erected a few months after the house was built, in Edwardian times, to help make them a more attractive prospect for potential purchasers. Now, with the railings gone, they would be reduced to privet or beech or laurel, acacia maybe, and it wouldn't be the same, not at all.

He sat at his desk watching the workers. Watching the boy especially. The youth took off his shirt in the boiling heat. The muscles pulled in his shoulders, his arms, his back, all in harmony, as he helped a colleague saw the remaining resistance out of the railings.

He was watching the youth so closely, that he realised he'd forgotten to be sorry about what was happening, the indignity being done to his home.

Moments later Mrs Harkness passed by, and Jennifer with her. Jennifer must have had the morning off from her school too. She looked over and spotted him at the window and waved a white-gloved hand at him. He hesitated for a few seconds before lifting his arm, opening his hand, slowly spreading his fingers like a fan. An immobile little wave. Maybe she was puzzled, because the smile seemed to slide on her face. He didn't smile back at her. That was bound to set her discussing him again in earnest with her friends. He knew he was a frequent topic of conversation: about how he wasn't more demonstrative when she asked him to dance with her at the tennis club socials. He was aware that some of the girls were trying to matchmake, pairing him off with her. He wasn't sure why he wasn't able to respond more openly. Stupid, really. But he just felt that – he couldn't. It hadn't to do with Jennifer, who was nice enough. He didn't dislike her. But sometimes he felt intimidated by her: the smell of talcum and shampoo, the paleness and warmth of her skin. Intimidated. And not anxious as some of his own friends were to discover what lay concealed behind the buttons of a girl's blouse.

He read a few more sentences from his history text-book, about Walter Raleigh and the English adventuring spirit. He read until he knew Jennifer and her mother would have passed. Then he raised his eyes again. He stared out at the youth: at the ease of his movements. He had grace, for all his – what his mother would have called commonness. He imagined him dressed in doublet and hose and ruff, gaze turned towards an Atlantic horizon, face in profile. Not a *fine* face, but handsome, in a rough and ready way.

He realised too late that his eyes had fixed to a stare, that the youth was watching *him*. How long had he been looking while making the resemblance to Walter Raleigh? He lowered his head . . .

When he had to go out, to return to school, after lunch, the railings in front of their own house and their neighbours' had gone. Only ugly stumps were left, which would have to be filed down. The workmen were now at the other end of the terrace. His mother was inspecting the damage.

'Whatever would your father have to say, Roy?'

His father wouldn't have let it worry *him*, because he wasn't the type to: in that respect, he was a careful foil to his mother.

'It'll be all right, Mum.'

He touched her arm sympathetically. She smiled, sadly, but was grateful nonetheless. He had a knack of knowing what would give her comfort.

'Wasn't that Mrs Harkness who passed by?' she asked.

'Was it?'

'Whatever will she think of us?'

His mother favoured Jennifer Harkness, because her

parents lived in a detached house with half an acre of garden. She kept telling him that good exam results would take him to university, that he would become qualified to enter a profession. She might have been expected to view Jennifer Harkness as a distraction: but quite the reverse. She seemed to belong to the scenario of his life that his mother had in mind for him. His glittering future.

He said goodbye to his mother, and walked along the terrace. When he reached the end and turned into the lane, the short-cut to the grammar school, he heard a quiet but distinct whistle from the verge. The youth was sitting in the shade of a thorn hedge. He was alone. His shirt was still off, his body seemed to have browned since the morning. 'Saw you looking,' he said. 'from your window back there. That your bedroom?' The voice was oddly rough and sweet at the same time. 'Like what you're looking at, then?' Roy turned away, so he wasn't looking, but the voice followed him. 'A quid, how'd that suit you? A quid, and you and me could go for a walk by the river.'

His head reeled. He shut his eyes. He heard the din of more railings being thrown on to the back of the lorry. Everything now – in a matter of moments – was being turned upside down, inside out. The voice was saying something else, under the screeching of metal. About it's taking one to know one . . . But he wasn't listening. Somehow he found the will to move off. To start walking. To put some distance, any distance, behind him.

Our privacy's gone, he was thinking, the world is opening up. This is not how I want it to be. Suddenly he understood his mother's worry about the railings. The vulgarity: showing themselves. At the end of the lane he was vaguely conscious of a familiar figure, Mrs Harkness without Jennifer, walking by on the other pavement. He smiled like a maniac, not towards her but into the middle of the road. What had the words spoken from the shade of the hedge *meant*? He knew, of course he did, but he wasn't thinking, wasn't thinking.

*

After that, Jennifer's friends began to look on him more indulgently as he allowed himself to show willing. He partnered her at tennis doubles. They practised together, and notched up a few significant wins for the club. He let her show him how to kiss. It felt awkward, unnatural even. But he learned how to, despite her talcumy smell clinging to his clothes, and the clutch of her hand on his sleeve paralysing his arm. From novels and a film or two he mastered the right words to say to her. He memorised and rehearsed the nice remarks of no consequence that would cause her mother to smile whenever he was invited to their house. He taught himself to swallow Mrs Harkness's monstrous dry-as-dust saffron cake between swigs of hot tea from the good china cups.

One Friday afternoon, in the year the King died and in the month Everest was conquered, he married Jennifer Harkness – like a mountaineer in the high ether, not thinking. Not thinking.

The big church on the High Street had kept its railings. And, on the day, children poked their faces between the bars and old women offered the newly-weds sentimental smiles.

But now his dream of the past would end.

Their life together had been quiet. He did decently well in the tax offices, but not outstandingly so. To the complacent eyes of the town Jennifer and he settled quite predictably into domesticity, the childless sort, and in the fullness of time Mrs Harkness's home became their own. Half the garden they sold to a builder, and then they were obliged to raise quick-growing conifers to minimise the hazard to their privacy.

Since Jennifer's death he had given more attention to those temptations he had kept so hidden from her for nearly forty years. In the new town he'd moved to – among strangers – he felt freer. But the predatory aspect was a long-standing habit by now. Unfortunately for him he took less care in how he went about the business of picking up.

He was apprehended by the police, in a public place. He told them, panicking, that it had never happened before, and he knew they didn't believe him. The police reminded him the youth was young enough to be his grandson. Did he have a family of his own? He answered no, and he considered it a blessing, although to Jennifer it had been a constant sorrow. Then he told them his bereavement had sent him off the rails. He supposed Jennifer would be turning in her grave to hear his lies, but he wasn't thinking any more. He wasn't thinking.

The prison is new, but nobody calls it that. He has been promised counselling. A psychiatrist breezily informed him that the problems lie inside, deep inside, and there they will find the solutions too. He hopes there will be no barriers to understanding, to truthfulness. All the time the man was smiling, he was emptying his pipe into a brass ashtray. Suddenly he was back, turning that corner again, from the terrace into the grassy lane, past the lorry of dead railings. The boy under the thorn hedge smiles up at him, slyly, as if he foresees the end of everything: you have to be honest or else. The railings go tumbling into the lorry's hold. Everyone talking of a better world ahead, one day when the War is over, talking of liberation, while all the time – clank, clank – a cage of iron was being cast and riveted around him.

THE DEATH OF THE ELMS

Georgina Hammick

Georgina Hammick has published two collections of short stories (*People For Lunch* and *Spoilt*) and has contributed to a number of literary journals and anthologies including *The Listener*, *Critical Quarterly*, *Writer's Tales* and *Best Short Stories*. She lives in Wiltshire.

'The Death of the Elms' was first broadcast on Radio 3, read by Diana Bishop.

THE DEATH OF THE ELMS

'Remember the elms? Remember what England was like before the elms died?'

Dickie asked me this out of the blue in the pub the other night, as we sat over our double whiskies – his fourth, my second. He was already at the maudlin stage, and any minute now he'd become aggressive – at which point, being a coward, I'd have to make some excuse about my husband needing me at home and leave. Dickie's in his seventies, and lonely since his wife died last year. We got talking when I came in for cigarettes one evening and he was at the bar. I stood there for what felt like an hour, leaning this way and that, waving, stupidly smiling, scowling, calling out 'Hi!' and 'Hallo there!' – every trick I could think of to get the barman's attention, a horrible business always – and eventually I turned to the old man at my elbow who was smiling into his glass, and said: 'S'all right for you, mate. Try being a woman sometime.' A mistake on my part, because Dickie jumped to at once, all charm and chivalry, and introduced himself, and raised one authoritative finger for the barman. And of course, when the barman came (within seconds, to prove my point), Dickie insisted on buying me a drink.

Since then, whenever Dickie and I coincide in the pub, I have to have a drink with him, and listen to him right the world, and hear about his genius grandchildren and how he won the war against Hitler single-handed. But on this occasion his subject was England, and how it used to look before they grubbed the hedgerows out and before the elm trees died. 'There was nothing to match them, you know,' he said mournfully, 'towering galleons, they were, peerless sentinels . . .' A tear fell and splashed into the puddle of lager

133

and cigarette ash, the legacy of some earlier occupants, on our table. 'Mind you, the government could've saved them if they'd wanted to. When you consider what science has managed in other areas ... but fact is, the buggers weren't prepared to pay, didn't consider it important. Usual story of apathy and incompetence. Or' – he took a swig of whisky, leant towards me, his purple face disconcertingly close to mine, and stage-whispered – 'it was something a lot more sinister. I'm inclined to suspect, young lady, that Dutch elm disease wasn't an accident at all. I'm tempted to believe the buggers imported the beetle on purpose to kill off the elms. Farmers never liked the trees, y'know. Treacherous, as they had it, hollow, easy fallers, a threat to farm buildings and machinery. If you want to know what I think' – Dickie stopped suddenly and sat back hard in his chair – 'but you don't want to know. A young thing like you, a Londoner like you, can't be expected to remember the elms. The loss of England's crowning glory can't mean anything to you.'

'Oh Dickie,' I said, 'what a lot of nonsense you talk.' For although I was a Londoner, and born there, I'm a farmer's wife now and have been for years. Dickie knows this because I've told him. And I'm not a young thing, I'm forty-three. I remember the elms; I lived in an elm landscape once.

The year the elms started to die I was teaching at a village school in Oxfordshire, my first job after teacher training college and my first experience of living out of London. The country was bad news, my friends had warned me, all mud and nettles; there was nothing to do there; the winters were terrible; if boredom didn't kill me, the cold would. That's what my friends said – and they were very nearly right about the cold – but I found I liked mud and nettles. Before I'd been in Oxfordshire a month I'd decided I was a country girl, deprived until now of her natural habitat. Even the day of my interview, perched on the stained back seat of the taxi on the ride from the station, head out of the window to catch the breeze, I had a sense of homecoming. It was August, hot and hazy with a white sky, and the feathery verges were spiked with thistle and ragwort. Giant elm trees, growing at intervals in the high-banked hedge, banded the lane with shadow, roofing it in places; and driving underneath I had the impression of a series of dusty black umbrellas held high over my head. I leaned out and looked up into those creaky, mysterious awnings, and breathed in the corn-stubble smell, and thought, I remember thinking: I'm going to get this job, and it'll be OK. I'll be OK here.

I did get the job, and it was OK. That first year I rented a small red cottage from a farmer. It was one half of a pair of semi-detached cottages, the only brick buildings in an otherwise stone village. Until July, when he was given the sack for stealing (wage packets, so I was told later), my cottage had been home to a cowman. Luckily for me, though, the farmer decided he could get by without another cowman, and he let me have the place on a temporary footing. He let me keep some furniture too, a bed, a deal table, an exhausted sofa with really savage springs, and a few kitchen oddments. Being bang on the road, the cottage had no front garden; but round the back, beyond the coal house and a concrete slab supporting pots of parched tomato plants, was a long strip of chaotic grass where I discovered a pear tree and a washing line and a collapsed wigwam of runner beans. At the very end of the strip, my side of the fence, grew two magnificent elm trees. I was excited by this bounty, especially by my elms which seemed too tall and grand for garden trees; and each daybreak, listening to the rooks arguing in their branches, I had that feeling of charged anticipation I remember as a child, on holiday once at the sea. By the time term started I'd painted all the inside walls white, and pinned up posters of landscapes by Monet and Cézanne; and cut the grass first with a scythe, and then with an old push mower I borrowed from my next-door neighbours, the Loughboroughs.

'Never fall out with a Dodwell, mind – yer'll get no meat, no milk and no beer if yer do,' Mrs Loughborough told me the week of my arrival. She laughed after she'd said it, but her laughter contained some resentment, I thought – understandable because you didn't need to be in the village a week to realise that the Dodwells dominated the community. Jack and Wendy ran the pub, Peter and Iris the shop, and Frank, a widower and dairyman, the milk round. Dead Dodwells took up most of the churchyard. Live Dodwells stood out from the village notice board, in the lists of parish and parochial church council members, and of the village hall and playing field committees. It was Dodwells – according to the judges of the Flower Show, at any rate – who grew the finest marrows and dahlias and who made the lightest sponge cake and the most flavoursome damson cheese. And when, on that first morning of the autumn term, I sat down at 'teacher's desk' in the Big Schoolroom and took the register, I found there were no fewer than five Dodwells in my class of twenty-three seven-year-olds.

'Dodwells've bin runnin things 'ere for nigh on four 'undred year,' Mrs Loughborough told me, adding sourly, 'an the way 'em breed, 'em'll be runnin things for the next four 'undred.'

Mrs Loughborough's prediction must have tempted fate, because not long after it handsome Peter Dodwell of the General Stores and Post Office abandoned his wife Iris and their six little ones and bolted to Plymouth, taking the profits (and the schoolgirl who'd been helping on the till on Saturdays) with him. Iris and the children caught the first ferry home to her parents in County Dublin; the shop was sold to pay off Peter's debts; and in no time at all the new owners, a Mr and Mrs Baldree, had moved in.

The Baldrees' names were Warren and Dawn, and they had a baby son, Adam. They'd come to the village from Birmingham, where Warren had owned a corner tobacconists and newsagents, and were at once labelled, though not to their faces, 'The Baldrees of Brum'. I'm not sure now if any outsider would have been allowed to make a real go of something that had been the province of the Dodwell clan. Warren Baldree, though, was tactless and opinionated from the start, refusing all advice and rearranging the shelves on the very first day in so arbitrary a fashion that natural neighbours, such as baked beans and tinned spaghetti, found themselves at opposite ends of the shop. He was over-familiar, and addressed even native born citizens by their first names without being invited. He talked big too, which nobody likes in newcomers. It was impossible to pop in for a box of matches without having to hear an account of his successes on the rugby field, or of the fast cars he'd driven, or what a whizz he was at snooker. (The stuff about fast cars especially hard to swallow, since the car he drove now was a rust-holed transit van with buckled doors.) I don't think anybody liked Baldree. Personality aside, he was unattractive in a dough-faced and heavy-jowled way, not improved, I thought by woolly sideburns that came down to his jaw. The hipster jeans and tight T-shirts he went in for did nothing to disguise a conspicuous beer stomach. What we all wanted to know was, why had Dawn married him? Anyone could see she was a nice girl, friendly but unpushy — and pretty too. Her eyes, especially, were arresting, dark and expressive. I used to think her nose spoiled her looks a little — it was too long and interfered with her top lip somehow — and I remember wondering, the first time I saw her, if it bothered her and whether she'd ever considered having it shortened, as I felt I might have done had it been mine.

In those days I did my food shopping, which never amounted to much (our school dinners, cooked on the premises by Mrs Kevin Dodwell, were harmless and substantial), on my bike journey home from work. Baldree would be at the till when I entered, dishing out opinions and small change; while Dawn washed the floor, which she did on her knees, or packed the delivery orders into boxes, checking each item off against a list. Beside her, in his pram-cum-pushchair, laughing and shouting and waving his fat little arms, would be the baby, Adam. He must have been around seven months then, very smiley with pink, tight cheeks and sweet breath and a lot of dark hair. He liked to grab the shoppers as they passed, and pull them down; and then, mouth open and with that frowning concentration babies have, play with their earrings or coat buttons — or, in my case, the painted wooden beads I invariably wore as being suitable for school.

'That Adam's a real time waster,' Mrs Loughborough confided – a compliment, for her – and I agreed. It was through
wasting so much time with Adam that I got to know Dawn.
She was a townie like myself; not twenty-one yet, she told
me, and I was surprised. Perhaps because she was married,
and a mother, I'd assumed she must be older than I was.

My cottage was a good half mile from the shop, up a
narrow lane known unofficially as Elm Avenue, and at closing
time, providing Dawn had finished her chores, she'd walk
back with me, wheeling my old black bike while I pushed
Adam in the pram. On fine days, we'd go via the playing field
and sit Adam down in the scrubby grass by the swings, while
the two of us sat on a bench and studied the fashion pages
of women's magazines, taking turns to choose the most out-
rageous get-ups we could find for the other to wear. We sang
a lot too – standards, old rock and roll numbers, hits from
the charts. Dawn was keen on Lynne Anderson's 'Rose
Garden', a big hit that year, which I considered mush. She
was always singing it. Sometimes when I was depressed, fed
up with school or life, waiting for a letter, she'd say to me in
a mock-solemn, mock-reproachful tone: 'I beg your pardon
– I never promised you a rose garden, you know.'

Dawn and I did these things together, we went for walks
and sat on benches and sang songs, but we never discussed
our personal lives. There was a cut-off point with her, I felt,
a reserve, that stopped me asking as I longed to ask, about
her marriage and why she'd done it, and whether she didn't
think Warren a monster really. It was monstrous to work a
young wife hard all day, as Baldree did, and then abandon
her each evening while he went drinking at the pub. She never
complained about it, but when I offered to babysit for Adam
she said 'Thanks, that'd be great', and after that Baldree did
take her out once in a while, on a Saturday, if I was free.

To tell the truth, I never enjoyed babysitting at the Baldrees
and only did it for Dawn. The living-room at the back of the
shop was low-ceilinged and dark, with only one small
window whose limp curtains refused to meet. There were no
pictures on the brown walls, no books, nothing in the way

of ornaments. It was a junk room really, full of cardboard boxes and crates of empty beer bottles, and it smelled of damp cardboard even in summer. In winter I had to stand over the paraffin stove in my overcoat in order not to freeze. Adam was generally asleep upstairs when I arrived. I never told Dawn this, but sometimes, if the telly wasn't working, I'd wrap Adam in a blanket and bring him down for company and sit him on my knee.

I'm not sure exactly when it was I noticed that the shop was going downhill – the shelves emptying, the customers staying away – but in my mind its decline coincides with two other events: Baldree putting himself on a diet (and boring us with all the details) and the sudden appearance, in the layby outside the shop, of a red two-seater sports car. The diet, we decided, was just another Baldree whim, not to be taken seriously. The car was real, though, a Triumph Sprite, and had been left to Dawn, a non-driver, by her uncle. We soon wished Dawn's uncle had had someone else to leave his car to, because Baldree was a menace in it, accelerating through the lanes at all hours and taking corners, and pedestrians, by surprise. He was warned repeatedly to cut his speed but, true to form, ignored the warnings.

About two months after the arrival of the new car, a Saturday in March, I was babysitting for Adam. Baldree usually took Dawn to our local on her evenings out, a short walk from the shop over the green, but on this occasion they were going to The Cross Keys, a roadhouse five miles away (it had a snooker table, which our pub didn't). I can see Dawn now, blowing me a kiss from the door. She was wearing the mini dress she wore to all village events – purple, with yellow cuffs and belt, very eye-catching. She'd done something new to her hair – flicked the ends up, I think – and I remember saying how nice it looked and how much it suited her, though I wasn't sure it did.

'Back about midnight,' Baldree called to me from the car, as I stood on the step to watch them go. He winked. 'Don't do anything I wouldn't do, and if you can't be good, be careful!'

They weren't back by midnight. Nor by one. Nor by two-thirty, and soon afterwards I fell asleep in my chair. At five when I woke there was still no sign of them. I knew I ought to ring the police, but couldn't bring myself to. So instead, I emptied the washing machine and hung the damp clothes on the airer, and then reloaded the machine with a pile of dirty stuff, jeans and so on which I found on the floor in the washroom. I got Adam up next, and he was in his highchair and messing about with his cereal when the policemen arrived. They told me that Baldree, very drunk, had got into a race with another sports car on the way home. The Sprite had left the road in Elm Avenue and hit a tree. Dawn and Baldree had both, as one of the policemen put it, 'sustained fatal injuries.'

Mrs Loughborough had it later that Dawn was still alive when the ambulance got there, and that she whispered 'I'm not going to die', over and over. I try not to think about that, and I pray it isn't true. At the time it didn't seem to make much difference. Dawn was dead, was all I cared about, and her husband had murdered her. I hated Baldree for years; but recently I've found myself feeling almost sorry for him. He was not unlike Dickie in a way. Also – what I forgot to mention – he did stick to that diet. He cut out fats and sugar and took up jogging, and he'd lost two stone at least when they hit the tree. There's something ironic and pathetic about that. I'm haunted by it, as I'm haunted by all those clothes in the washroom – those dirty clothes they'd worn the day before. The clean ones, I hung up, they'd never wear.

I wanted to adopt Adam. But of course, not having a husband then, and on only a trainee teacher's pay, I wasn't considered a good bet. There was a lot of local rivalry to adopt him, and feelings got heated in the final stages. In the end Jack and Wendy Dodwell of the pub were the lucky ones. They changed Adam's surname when they took him over, so he's a Dodwell now.

One of the worst things after Dawn was killed, was having to see the elm tree Baldree drove her into. It was just a few yards from my door, and for weeks I went around with my eyes shut to avoid that mangled, and magnetic, trunk. A tree specialist from the council turned up eventually, and tarred the lacerated bark; but the elm died after a couple of months.

I didn't tell Dickie this the other night because he never listens, and because he has his own theory anyway about the elms – but it was about the time they felled the wounded tree, in June, that the leaves of the elms at the end of my garden began to look sick, and to turn yellow, and to fall. And it was soon after that, as I remember, that all the elms in England started to die, one by one by one.

THE LUNCH BOX

Gillian Tindall

Gillian Tindall is the author of many novels and works of non-fiction. Her novels include *Fly Away Home* (winner of the Somerset Maugham Prize), *The Intruder* and most recently *Spirit Weddings*. She has published three short story collections and is now writing an historical book on The Berry region in France. She lives in London.

'The Lunch Box' was first broadcast on Radio 4, read by Anna Massey.

THE LUNCH BOX

Umé's mother kept dreaming about her daughter's lunch box. She did not mention the dream to anyone because, although it worried her, it seemed too silly. In these times people had worse things than lunch boxes on their minds. Many of them, those who were refugees from other cities which had suffered much more from bombs than this one had, woke muttering, shaking or crying out from dreams that came from their immediate experiences. This, Umé's mother couldn't help thinking, seemed to make nonsense of the old superstition that dreams of fire or death are actually a good omen because dreams go by opposites. But these days so many of the traditions and superstitions had been swept away.

Umé's mother supposed that she dreamed of the lunch box because it was such a worry finding something to put in it. But, really, that was far from being her greatest worry, or one peculiar to her. Most things were in short supply these days and everyone was in the same boat. The war was not going well; that much was clear, in spite of the official line on 'keeping a firm purpose'. She worried much more about her eldest son, far away in the army, and about her younger son, only in High School but drafted already for Civil Defence work: able-bodied men were in short supply as well as food.

She did not need to worry about her husband because he was employed at a factory in the city. But she did worry, all the same, that the strain of the times wouldn't do his asthma any good. It had been worse recently, though it usually improved in the summer.

She also worried about her brother and his wife and their two children, who had arrived several months ago in a sorry state from the port city where their own home had been destroyed in the bombing. They, thank goodness, had recently left to spend a holiday with the old people in the country – 'thank goodness' because although, as family, they had been more than welcome, they had made the little house feel very crowded and catering for that number had been a problem.

So, really, now of all times, when her own situation had eased a little, why should she be having bad dreams about Umé's lunch box?

Bad dreams – yes. For that was what they were. This was another reason she couldn't mention them to anyone. How to explain that, in the night-world where everything was the same yet different, the lunch box figured with some particular formless dread attached to it. Such a harmless little tin box, like thousands of others. It had a carrying strap and irises stamped and painted on the lid. In her dream the box was monochrome grey all over – but then she had heard it said that one does not dream in colour. The imprint of the irises was still clearly recognisable. The boxes were made locally in a factory that now turned out hand-grenade casings. Why should a school-girl's lunch box be so terrifying that Umé's mother should wake in the mornings in horror – horror that, a few seconds later, was drenched in grief?

She got up as soon as she woke these days – it was a relief to do so – and busied herself quietly with household duties before her husband and children were awake. In the very early mornings at this time of year the heat was less oppressive and the sky was clear all the way to the mountains. She watered plants in pots, put other water on to boil, spread out fresh shirts, tried to plan food for the day. Sometimes their neighbour, a widower, would be up and about in his yard. And he and she would exchange conversation in muted tones over the fence: the temperature, news from other cities, the good old days. She really preferred that last as a subject of conversation. Their neighbour had grown to manhood in a previous era and had a reassuring, ceremonial way of talking about life and the passing years. She liked to think that, being old, he could take a more balanced view of present events. It cheered her, a little, that he did not seem as anxious as some people were. He had great faith, he said, in High Command; they knew what they were doing. The great thing was to stick honourably to your post and never show that you were afraid: cowards brought defeat on themselves by talking about it.

She knew that the last remark was straight from the wireless but somehow it comforted her more coming from her neighbour's lips. Before he retired he had had a most worthy career in the general post office: he must know what he was talking about. Anyway, he reminded her a little of her father.

One bright morning – even before seven it promised to be another very hot day – she found herself confiding in him about her dream. Or, at least, she had meant to confide her dream. But it was as if the dream itself possessed some power which made it impossible to divulge clearly. Instead, she found herself hesitating, feeling for words, and then saying that she was at her wits' end for something to put in Umé's lunch box. She hadn't meant to say this at all. It was a ridiculous complaint to make to a man. The kitchen was not their department. And she knew as she said it that a retired civil servant from the post office could not be expected to concern himself about these things: his sister-in-law called in daily to cook for him. But out it came, all the same. Her husband was able to eat in his factory canteen, which of course was a great saving, and there was a canteen now for the Civil Defence boys near the main tram depot – but Umé? Umé must still be provided with something for the long hours away from home. Something light but sustaining. The child was not strong. The doctor examining Umé at the beginning of the year had talked of her needing more 'protein', but where, for goodness sake, could a mother get protein in these days? Umé had been growing fast. What a pity children could not stay quiescent in hard times, like flowers in winter, and only attempt further development in a favourable season. What a pity their eldest son had had to become a man at this time and be sent into danger far from his mother and his home

. . . But no, one mustn't think like that. It was disloyal and cowardly . . .

'But I mustn't bore you with my silly little problems,' she said to the old man, beginning to back away. 'After all, we're all in the same boat.'

She retreated indoors, and tried to distract herself by waking the others five minutes before it was necessary to do so. But a little later, while her husband was going through his usual gargling and spitting rituals at the sink on the end of the porch, she came outside again to spread the quilts for airing and found her neighbour stationed by the fence as if he had been waiting for her. He beckoned to her, and pressed a box into her hand.

'Just a few savoury biscuits my nephew brought last time he was on leave. I was saving them but I really don't know what for. Your little girl might as well have them. They're tasty and quite – what was the word you used? – sustaining. See, there's enough for several days here.'

She could hardly find the right words to thank him. Exchanging presents was all part of the proper way of life – people did it all the time, even now – but she understood that this was a true gift, made from pure kindness, and that he did not want any return. How good human nature was really, in spite of everything! She tried to tell him so, but he became embarrassed and waved her away. She returned to her own house, flustered but elated, to feed them their usual breakfast. She would only tell Umé about the biscuits, as a nice surprise, when the child was setting off, a little later than the others. Husbands, sons, brothers and fathers normally got the best of everything, and that was no doubt right, but it was lovely, once in a while, to be able to give a little treat to one's only daughter.

When they had gone their several ways, with the usual morning flurry of urgency, she sat down on the step of the porch for a few minutes' rest before embarking on the bulk of the housework. A dragonfly came skimming past her and hovered over the last blooms of the potted hydrangea, the sun glinting on its wings. She followed it with her tired eyes, thinking what a delicate, pretty thing it was and, thinking this, fell abruptly asleep again for a few minutes – or at least, so she surmised when she woke with a start and an exclamation from another of Those Dreams. But not quite: this time the dream had not been so much horrible as simply mystifying and extraordinarily vivid.

She had been walking in the city, somewhere near the wide, green river. She knew it to be this same city, in the matter-of-fact way one does know things in dreams, but it seemed like somewhere quite other. The houses were different. And the streets. And it was all much more open. She kept getting glimpses between trees and lawns of the river which she knew was really lined with offices and wharves at this point. Their own district was near at hand but she couldn't even find the main road with the tramline which should lead to it.

She went on and, by and by, was inside a very large, light, cool building. There were other people there but she seemed to be on her own. She moved as if within her own mind, without physical effort, from one room to another and presently found herself standing looking down at a row of glass display cases for small objects, such as they have in museums.

And there, once again, lay Umé's lunch box, without its strap or paint, dull-grey all over as she had already seen it but with one end slightly buckled, as if it were a block of ice cream that had begun to melt.

This time, it was lying with its lid half off as if to display the contents. Small, close-packed, blackened flakes that might once have been biscuits. Or anything else, really. She bent low over the glass, studying it as if it could tell her something.

This was the point at which she woke again with an unpleasant jump and some unrecoverable word on her lips. What?

She was sweating as she sat there on the step. The sun must be getting hot. She could see the wall clock in the house from here; not yet much past eight. How long had she dozed? Only a few minutes. She felt as confused as if she had slept for many hours.

149

The dragonfly had gone. The crickets were beginning to chirp as usual in the neighbour's almond tree. After a while she got shakily to her feet.

Then, her eye was caught by another delicate aerial object. The sun glinted off it, and for a moment she took it for another garden insect, but then realised it was much further off, up in the sky above the city. It was a small parachute, floating gently downwards in the summer air, with something suspended below.

Just before she entered the house she saw the parachute descending slowly, peacefully, towards the centre of the city. The name of the city was Hiroshima.

BRAHMS INTERMEZZO (NR 118)

Irene Dische

Irene Dische is an American resident in Berlin. She has published a novel *Pious Secrets* and most recently a collection of short stories *The Jewess*.

'Brahms Intermezzo (NR 118)' was first broadcast on Radio 3, read by Liza Ross.

BRAHMS INTERMEZZO (NR 118)

When Mrs Herfort saw and heard what was happening on her fireplace mantelpiece she was astonished but not shocked. She wrested a chair from the living-room table (they resisted separation, clinging with their legs) and sat down in front of the fireplace to watch. Her husband had always referred to the object as a toy, but in fact, it was a calendar clock, covered with a glass dome. Inside this dome a ballerina pirouetted on a pedestal to a tinny melody. The porcelain doll wore a red bodice and white skirt. Her short hair was black, her cheeks and mouth red, but the rest of her hard hollow flesh was white. Mrs Herfort's surprise gave way to satisfaction.

Beneath the ballerina's pedestal, two sets of cardboard squares hinged on separate turnstiles. The glossy cards were marked in black, one with the first three letters of the month, the other with a number. One of each faced forwards, and the combination now read NOV 8 – although it was actually the beginning of May. The ballerina began to slow down. Finally she came to a halt, her accompaniment ending mid-melody with a ping. Invisible cogs whirred while the numbered card swung around, exposing the number behind it. NOV 9. The ticking, barely audible over the dance music, continued. Forty-seven years ago – the day had been recorded by the clock, the year remembered – the owner had smashed this expensive curio to the floor in a rage – his older brother had called him a sissy for being so fond of the little dancing lady inside. He was twelve and determined to enjoy the loud jangling noise she made when she broke. Then the glass dome had been mended and the ballerina restored without apparent scars. But that night the boy cried himself to sleep because

153

the clock no longer ticked. And the lady no longer danced to her music.

Exactly an hour after his death, almost five decades later, the ballerina came to life again, just at the time Mrs Herfort, freshly widowed, passed by her row-house fireplace. She didn't mistrust her senses. Faced with the implausibility of her widowhood, Mrs Herfort would have believed anything.

Anything? Although Mrs Herfort could accept the new ticking and the outbursts of tinny music in her living-room, she didn't believe in her husband's death. Certainly she knew that he was gone. Yet she left his plaid bedroom slippers standing by the bed and the torsos of his wardrobe hanging loosely on their closet hangers. Dr Herfort had often gone on business trips without her – once he had even forgotten his bedroom slippers – and he had always returned. Now his widow just couldn't make herself unhappy.

Her friends didn't realise how she felt about her loss. Most of them were middle-aged too but as yet untutored in the emotional nuances of mourning. They tried unconsciously to preserve this innocence, and while they poked around in her misfortune like tourists, they protected themselves with clichés. They turned out dutifully to watch her cry at her husband's funeral. They would have been appalled if they had guessed the real reason behind her spattering of tears.

At the gathering in her living-room after the funeral, Mrs Herfort puzzled everyone by eating a large helping of her neighbour's strawberry shortcake. She thanked her company for coming, and kicked off her new pinching black pumps with relief before the last guests had left. She seemed to be settling into her bereavement without any problems. She had no more rings than usual under her black eyes; her grey hair hadn't turned white overnight. She hadn't lost a pound of her slender figure. The morning after the simple service, she appeared at the music school of their town and rather forcefully requested a job in the library. She had lots of experience, she assured the head librarian, who was unnerved by Mrs Herfort's black spring suit. Under the circumstances, the librarian wanted to be helpful: she said it was high time someone sorted out the rarely used Basement Collection. Her assistants hissed to each other that it was a crime to send a widow into such gloomy surroundings. But Mrs Herfort didn't seem to mind.

Mrs Herfort had enjoyed the company of closed books since she was nineteen – when she studied library sciences on the advice of her husband. She had appeared an ordinary young woman when she had first met him in a neighbourhood church. It was luck, everyone said, a queer piece of luck that she had met someone who appreciated her. Because she seemed not to care terribly about having friends or finding a boy-friend. Everyone knew she loved music, although few knew how much.

Her father, a music teacher, had seen his daughter's talent when she was five. He bought her a quarter-sized violin and expensive lessons. At first she played precociously, but by the time she was ten her progress had been stifled by her own peculiar gift. Although the child was even-tempered, she responded like an instrument to the emotions of music: chills played up and down her spine, she would shiver violently, giggle and cry. When she was older, she could suppress these reactions; but then her hypersensitivity to music took on other forms. She tried to explain to her father about the 'places'. Every piece of music had its own visual manifestation: a stormy sea or a crowded ballroom, a jungle, or a market place. And as she listened, this vision acquired substance: she felt bodily drawn into the scene she pictured, while the room around her became distant and dim. When she mentioned this to her father he snapped that if she concentrated on musical structure, she'd stop seeing things. His irritation scared her and soon she put her violin away for good. But her relationship to music only grew queerer after she stopped playing. Her reactions were more extreme. Yet in other ways she remained quite normal, undemanding, and with few interests.

She had a job as a salesgirl in a music shop the year she met her future husband. She lived at home; the weeks marked by the Friday evening concerts at a nearby church. She always sat in the back of the choir, where no one could observe or distract her, and the organist stayed discreetly turned away. One night a young man, others would surely have called attractive, joined her there. He sat in a front pew and read a book about infectious diseases during the performance. The rustle of pages turning at odds with the tempo and, perhaps too, his maleness irritated her. The next week he returned and she didn't mind as much. On the third Friday, he slid into the rear aisle next to her. Again he leafed through a thick volume, looking up only once to smile at her, shyly. 'I always see you here,' he said after the programme ended. She agreed. They shared the same pew three times more before going out together afterwards for an ice-cream. At the local café, he explained that music helped him study. He was an internist. After that evening they started meeting elsewhere.

The progress of their relationship was slow but reliable. Dr Herfort was the son of a minister, and his sunny looks concealed a stolid nature. He grew fond of his girl-friend at the same rate that his father drank alcohol in public, taking incremental sips, never allowing his enjoyment to show. And he soon observed how music affected her otherwise sensible character. Gently, he persuaded her to give up her job at the music store where she stood dazed and dreaming at the cash register when the Victrola played. She studied library sciences instead, and worked in the hospital library until the advent of Muzak in the elevators. Then she stayed home. The couple never went to another organ concert. After they were married, Dr Herfort banned her radio from the house.

It was at his funeral several decades later that Mrs Herfort's irrationality – as her husband had identified it – appeared again. She didn't cry at the eulogy. When his colleagues ticked off a list of the dead man's polysyllabic virtues, her eyes remained dry. It was after the sermon that Mrs Herfort broke down, when the organist played the most glorious Bach prelude bringing her to open ocean, with each variation of the theme rippled in the water. Hearing and seeing such beauty, tears poured from Mrs Herfort's eyes, splashing down her cheeks and into her black collar. Her sister helped her out of the stall.

The next day, Mrs Herfort arrived in the music school library, umbrella sensibly in hand, and tapped the stick on the floor while the librarian considered her widow's outfit.

It was a rainy May morning when Mrs Herfort assumed her duties as Third Assistant Librarian. She began by sorting out the Reger collection in the basement stacks. The books were mouldering, their sheaves damp. Mrs Herfort dusted the bindings tenderly and caressed certain pages as if she could feel the notes. She had just slid the last book back into its ranks when she heard, distantly, Brahms' Second Intermezzo Op. 118. Someone was practising in a room overhead. Sieved through the floor, the piece had the full flowing lines which her imagination restored to them.

Mrs Herfort wrung her hands.

She leaned heavily against a bookcase, indifferent to the track of dust on her black suit. An image had come to her with the music: a tree with high sweeping branches. The leaves were the opulent dark green of late summer. They hung still, the sun scattering through them.

Upstairs, she casually asked a student at the check-out desk, 'Who is that playing Brahms?'

'Oh, that. That must be Hugo Atteliades. The little Greek. He's from Athens.'

The next day, Mrs Herfort met Hugo as he was leaving his regular practice room. She had been leaning against the door eavesdropping, when he suddenly slammed down the piano top and snapped 'Open the door,' so that she almost tumbled inside.

It was not at all like Mrs Herfort to adopt a stranger as a friend. She had no reason to do so now because she wasn't lonely. Dr Herfort's presence lingered and silence had been characteristic of him. In fact, the couple had never been in the habit of telephoning each other when he was away. Dr Herfort had been a reasonable man, his wife a stalwart woman. 'The only one who loses if we don't speak to each other for a few days is the telephone company,' he liked to say. She had agreed, telling herself there was romance in separation. So when Dr Herfort left his wife for good she accepted his absence without protest. She even had the company of the calendar clock and the dancer who had spun to life with her boxed song. The clock hadn't recovered its usefulness. It couldn't adjust to contemporary time – the mechanical knob that might have turned the calendar back to the appropriate date had snapped off – and so it read NOV 12 when outside the glass 15 May was the prevailing date. And the dancer heeded only the rhythm of her metal heart, which prompted her midnight dance at 2.17 every afternoon. Mrs Herfort took a late lunch break at home so she could watch the ballerina pirouette and one calendar leaf give away to another. No, Mrs Herfort wasn't lonely. And, now she had Hugo.

The friendship had begun the day she made his acquaintance. Hugo hadn't minded that someone stumbled away when he'd opened his practice-room door. 'Pardon me,' he had mumbled in a heavy accent and stepped back to see what the stranger would do next. He was a foreign exchange student, a clever, domineering boy who was thoroughly intimidated by America.

She was charmed by him. Even as she stumbled at the threshold. She noticed with pleasure his slenderness, his olive skin, his ruined teeth and fleshy nose which was clamped by a pair of black spectacles. Later she saw that his hands were beautiful, with small palms and long fingers, a half moon in each nail. After she complimented Hugo on his playing, he invited her in for a private recital. She sat on a chair behind him, where she could see his hands flap into view at either end of the keyboard. He played Chopin. The small lamp at the piano turned him into a giant shadow slanting across the bare windowless room. He sat stiffly, with a rounded back, and every so often, when the tension of playing became too much for him, gasped through clenched teeth. How distracting, thought Mrs Herfort gratefully.

But when he began again the Brahms Intermezzo she lost control of herself. The cramped walls of the practice room with the pianist's hideous shadow faded. The small light burning over his hands became ghostly, and she saw in their place a late-summer tree, absolutely motionless, with sunlight glazing every leaf.

Mrs Herfort felt faint. She thought of her husband.

'Hugo,' she interrupted. He stopped playing and looked back at her. 'I forgot!' she shook her head, 'I forgot, in the library . . .' and she stepped out of the door.

But she returned the next day. And the next. She was drawn to the Greek boy with the beautiful hands and the singular face, drawn to his music, and perhaps something else. Throughout that week they remained strangers, barely speaking. But every afternoon she slipped up from the basement stacks and he performed for her. He always paused before beginning the Intermezzo, sensing her excitement. She surrendered herself to the music, while the bare room grew dimmer, and she revelled in her vision of a tree heavy with greenery while far away a yellow field led to a yellow sun.

As the long week after Dr Herfort's death came to an end, and she had still not cried for her loss, Mrs Herfort broke her customary silence with Hugo. She invited him to the movies. He accepted, with grave formality. That night they met on Main Street in front of a brightly-lit cinema featuring a cowboy film. She paid for his ticket, she bought him candy, and enjoyed herself enormously, as did he, if his awkwardly loud laughter was any indication. But midway through the film she could no longer concentrate. She suddenly, inexplicably dreaded the moment she would no longer be sitting with him in the dark. But it was not so bad afterwards. He walked her home, shook her hand, and if she held on for longer than was common courtesy he did not shake her off, or even seem to notice. Later, at home, she made herself comfortable in her solitude, sitting in the living-room, allowing the quiet heartbeat of the calendar clock to comfort her.

The next day, ten days into her widowhood, Mrs Herfort watched the ballerina dance as usual and the calendar flip its page to NOV 18. Mrs Herfort ignored the pleasant spring weather as she rushed back to the library – her eyes still dry as she descended gladly into the gloom of the library basement.

At 4 o'clock the ceiling above registered Hugo's arrival. Shortly afterwards Mrs Herfort knocked at his door. When Hugo opened it Mrs Herfort noticed that he was somehow changed: he looked at her with an expression she could not interpret. She thought perhaps she had come too soon but he gestured her with a nod to her chair. Instead of performing for her, though, he continued to practise a Chopin ballad. Again and again he broke off in the middle of a phrase and picked up somewhere else in the piece, to her distress. Just as she was thinking she should return to work, Hugo glanced back at her with a small smile and began the Brahms Intermezzo, Op. 118. Now the pianist performed. And today it seemed that he played more irresistibly than ever. She saw the tree and how its leaves began to tremble. She noticed the silvery undersides of the leaves as the music appeared to ruffle them. She stood up and moved to the piano, the source of the sound, and put her hand on Hugo's shoulder.

But abruptly he stopped playing and stood up with a jerk, slapping her hand off. His eyes registered fear and malice.

Mrs Herfort turned and ran. She burst out of the dark library, scuttling along the sidewalk, but the Intermezzo moved with her, roaring in her ears while the weight of the tree's foliage seemed to press around her. When she reached home, stepping over the threshold, the harmony of the Intermezzo slipped into something she no longer recognised and then the tree branches flinched in an icy wind.

It was a black wind with black wings that suddenly flayed the tree so that its branches lashed at each other and – at the crying of a chord – the leaves all turned black: the black of mourning cloth. And the leaves began to fall. First a few, then more, then finally a black blizzard, leaving the branches bare and white as bones. Mrs Herfort stepped into her living-room.

The ballerina clock had stopped ticking.

Brahms Intermezzo (Nr 118)

Mrs Herfort lay face down on the floor and wept into the carpet. Now, finally, she wept, wept for her loss, wept that her husband was gone and that her feelings for him were without resonance.

ABROAD

Peter Regent

Peter Regent was born in Suffolk and lives in Fife, where he writes and makes sculpture. Apart from Radio 4, his stories have appeared in periodicals, in his collection *Laughing Pig* and also in the Scottish Arts Council/Collins anthologies. He is currently working on a second collection of stories and a novel.

'Abroad' was first broadcast on Radio 4, read by Nigel Anthony.

ABROAD

Perpetua snorted upper-class laughter, uncrossed her sturdy legs, and crossed them again the other way with a squeak of nylon. The Major sat bolt upright, his cheeks spotted turkey-red, his neck reared from his semi-stiff collar.

'No', he said.

Like a family of owls, the members of the Board turned to where the Major and I sat together. Sir William had asked the Major to leave the room for the next item and he had refused:

'I'm not going while that girl's sitting there.'

'But Major,' growled Sir William, 'Miss Yarborough has to take the minutes – it's her job.'

'She has no business hearing you discuss my salary behind my back.'

Perpetua giggled. Her thighs whistled an arpeggio as she began to get up, but Sir William told her to stay where she was. An old sailor, he loosed a quarter-deck roar and the Major, stiffly erect, left the room. A week later, by his own choice, he left altogether.

I was sorry, because the Major had been the only other male employee of the Society, unless you counted the care-taker, who emerged from the basement twice a day to hoover the stairs and collect things for post. Sir William dropped in only occasionally to issue directives and inspiration. The rest – the Secretary, the Librarian, the Information Officer, the switchboard operator and Perpetua – were women. I got on with them all, but – well, a fellow likes a bit of male company.

The Major could afford good tweeds and the impracticality of suede shoes. He never swanked, though his passing refer-ences to the garden at Cheam suggested that it was extensive, and he arrived each day in a good car, even if it wasn't the latest model. He was a cheerful soul, and debonair as old soldiers often are. In his company I felt respectable, somehow. He was a retired Marine, and our accountant.

We were a registered charity. We earned a little from our publications, members contributed what they could, and Sir William had a flair for catching company chairmen at the right moment. The Major recorded all that and drew from uncertain reality a statement of order and balance, with a modest provision for wages. None of us was paid very much.

Our office overlooked the Thames. As the lowing of ship's sirens came drifting up-river from the docks, anyone passing the Major's door night have heard him murmur 'Turning to port . . .' or 'Turning to starboard . . .' according to the number of blasts. Sometimes he sang as he worked. Afterwards he always explained that he had been 'casting a trial balance'. He did that surprisingly often.

He and I didn't see much of each other, but every few days he would poke his head round my door to propose lunch at the nearby pub. The Major would munch his beef-with-mustard and explain how working in a place like ours was 'like being a Marine officer on a destroyer – "Good old Guns" when they want something, and "that bloody Pongo" the rest of the time'. He despaired of the state of the Nation: 'The only thing to do's to go abroad. Some little place in the Dordogne or Tuscany. Decent wine, decent food, the odd girl to help out . . . Spent most of my life abroad, of course. Can't wait to get back.'

And now the Major had gone, and with him the smell of good leather and tobacco and his aura of decency and sea breezes. The frayed carpet, the dusty walls and the grubby paintwork of the office reasserted themselves; the place was no longer the haunt of a gentleman.

The Major's successor was small and plump, vaguely middle-aged with indefinite, rubbed-out features that always wore an ambiguous smile. He smiled indiscriminately – at the telephonist, the caretaker, the milkman, Sir William and me. And as he smiled he murmured, in his slow voice, that yes, he was settling in all right; yes, the work was simple, compared with what he had been used to; yes, yes, of course.

When I took him to the pub for lunch, he ate his sandwich slowly, sipping at his half-pint, saying very little. I tried to make conversation, and said I was thinking of a trip abroad – to Italy, perhaps. That set him off. Italy? Yes, the exchange looked good, but one must remember that inflation was still very high. 'Yes, they're very outgoing, the Italians, but the Spanish are cleaner – at least, that's my opinion. They've put in all sorts of facilities on the Costa del Sol, and its very popular nowadays.' I mentioned Greece. 'Greece? Well, I always think the classical tour's what it's all about, unless you're very young. If it's just sun and sea you want, the west of Crete's the best bet – down on the south coast, preferably. But you know, the Algarve's so clean. Lovely beaches. All that fish, and more people speaking English every year. Then there's Southern Turkey . . .'

I marvelled at his familiarity with so many places. He smiled and murmured that he had done his travelling some time ago, before packaged tourism really got started. All the same, yes, he'd knocked about a bit.

But there were no accounts ready when the AGM came round. Sir William roared again, and the little man vanished. Afterwards, Sir William showed me the drawers stuffed with vouchers, the blank pages of the ledgers, and the day-books hidden under the piles of unanswered letters. As always, he seemed to relish disaster.

'The little blighter never did a thing,' he chuckled, opening a filing cabinet and spilling a deluge of paper.

In an alcove behind the door I found a coat. Its tweed was too good for the little man. 'It must be the Major's,' I said. 'We'll have to return it . . . You know, he quite liked sorting things out – casting trial balances and that sort of thing . . .'

'Any port in a storm. Can't afford to be stuffy. Try him,' said Sir William. He opened another drawer: 'My God! So that's how the little blighter spent his time!' He brooded over the drawer's contents: 'Crying, you know, when he left. Suppose I ought to do something about it, really.'

Perpetua afterwards told me Sir William was as good as his word. He was a patron of the arts, and he fixed the little man a job with Dalziel's gallery, where he often bought pictures. It wasn't much – nothing involving money, of course; mainly behind-the-scenes work – packing, stacking, labelling and that sort of thing.

The Major came back on a temporary basis, with a minimum of condescension. 'Poor little devil,' he said, looking into the drawer over which Sir William had brooded. 'Never lived, you see.'

He slammed the drawer shut and began to marshal vouchers and cashbooks on the desk. 'I'll need Perpetua to give a hand with this lot.' He picked up the telephone and I left him to it. On the stairs I passed Perpetua, whistling her stockings down to his room, and by the end of the week I heard him singing over his first trial balance.

A few months later, Sir William recommended the exhibition at Dalziel's. 'Nice to see real painting for a change.' So the next time I was in Bond Street I slipped into the gallery to look round. It was a high-class place, redolent of men's cologne and, more faintly, of turpentine. The pictures were hung in perfect order on pale linen walls, meticulously labelled with a card that was aligned exactly with the bottom of each frame. Everything proclaimed that this was a serious establishment: none of your whitewashed walls with pictures hung anyhow and a leggy girl filing her nails behind a desk in the corner. As I worked my way round, the staff nodded discreetly, then got on with murmuring to New York or Rome on the telephone. The prices on the labels were enormous.

'Hello Edward.' A familiar, purring tone. It was the little man, in a smarter suit than he had worn at our place, and with hair a good deal longer than Sir William would have cared for. I asked how he was getting on, and he found time to assure me that he liked his new job very much, before hurrying his smile across to a regular client. The gallery manager, seeing me abandoned, and knowing I was connected with Sir William, strolled over.

'Enjoying the show?'

'Nice to see real painting for a change.'

'It is rather fun, isn't it?' The manager's eyes were wandering over my shoulder. I made a bid for more attention:

'How's the new man settling in?'

'Very well – very well indeed.'

'I didn't realise he'd be part of your sales staff.'

'Well, he's not, strictly speaking, but we don't make a big thing of the distinction. Downstairs staff often bring up pictures for customers to see. Lord Meldrum rather took to him, and asked for him next time he came in. Now he's got a nice little group of clients of his own. It's been rather useful, what with Henry in the States and Richard in Bahrain.'

The manager lent an ear to a dapper little man who had come to breathe a message into it. 'We've sold the Rape of Helen? Splendid, Henry. How was New York?'

'Wonderfully exciting', said Henry. 'But I've got to take Lady Monica for lunch, and she'll insist on wine. I hate that, at midday.'

As Henry minced his little suit away I felt I could have put up with lunching Lady Monica, wine and all. A trip to New York wouldn't have come amiss, either: 'You all seem to do quite a lot of travelling.'

'It's a bore, but there's no avoiding it. We all have to do our whack. Did Gordon tell you he's going to Rome?'

'Gordon?'

'Gordon Tebbit.'

Of course, the little man was called Mr Tebbit. It had never occurred to me that he might have a Christian name. Going to Rome, indeed!

The Manager fluttered off. 'Give my love to Sir William,' he called, over his shoulder. 'Tell him I'll be in touch when I get back from Morocco.'

At the door Gordon Tebbit was ushering his clients out. He extended his smile to include me. 'Enjoy Rome,' I said,

169

and was astonished by the consternation that flooded his face. But he re-established his smile almost instantly: 'Well, one's been there before, of course . . .'

As I walked away I thought how clever Sir William had been, to land the little fellow so neatly on his feet. And in Gucci slippers, too.

Half-way through the next morning the gallery manager phoned. 'You've heard about the accident? It was in all the papers. Look, I'd rather not go into it on the phone, but it's about Tebbit. The police are here, and I'd be grateful if you'd come round . . . Well, right away if that's convenient.'

I rang Sir William, but he was in his bath, so I asked the Major to come with me. As he pushed open the plate-glass door of the gallery the Major twitched his moustache: 'I'm quite looking forward to meeting this Tebbit chap.'

'Well you can't,' said the Manager, who was waiting just inside. 'He's hung himself.'

'Too bad,' said the Major. His calm was remarkable – but then, slaughter had been his business.

'It's been perfectly dreadful,' continued the manager. 'Police everywhere, and our clients don't care for that at all. We haven't sold a thing all morning!'

'What happened?'

'Its all over the papers, by now. The first I heard was when I had a call from Rome asking why he hadn't arrived there. Then I came in and found him. He'd done it downstairs, after the rest of us had gone home. He'd even cancelled the burglar alarms – anyone could have got in!'

I imagined a plump little corpse rotating slowly in the picture store, goggling at startled nymphs and puzzled highland cattle. The manager looked at his watch. 'I think the police would like you to take a look at some things he left. They can't trace any next-of-kin or anything. Besides, we do rather need the desk.' He took us into the gallery and introduced us to an Inspector, who asked questions about Tebbit's time with us, then led the way to a rosewood davenport and opened the drawers, one by one.

The first contained picture-labels, a book of sales invoices, and the usual clutter of felt pens, paperclips and sticky tape. The next was full of our stuff, but there was nothing of any value. The Major flicked the pages of a couple of books we had published years before, lingering for a second over photographs of naked African girls and pieces of sculpture. Apart from that there were only a few pamphlets and some reference books from our library. None of it shed light on Tebbit's death.

'Then there's this,' said the Inspector. He opened the last drawer, and at the first gaudy flash I knew what it contained. The Inspector strewed the desk with dazzling blue skies and translucent bays set with elegant yachts, with fun in the surf and jollity in the disco. There must have been a year's crop of travel brochures. We sighed, and were sorry we couldn't be of more help.

'I wonder,' said the Major, as he led me to his club for lunch, 'if that poor devil had ever been further than Victoria.'

'I thought he'd travelled a lot. He was always talking about it.'

'What about that passport?' the Major demanded. The passport had been in the drawer too. Blue and gold, and crisp as a naval uniform. It was quite new.

At the Major's club one ate lamb cutlets or steak-and-kidney pudding, unless one was a foolish foreigner, who might order Vienna steak. The portraits in the dining-room glowered down on the black-stockinged waitresses like the castles in Tebbit's brochures frowning over licentious beaches. The Major hung over his cutlet.

'I'm leaving you at the end of the week,' he said. 'I would have given your next man a few days in double harness, but it's doctor's orders. Called in for a re-fit.' He took a sudden decision, stabbed a chop with his fork, and sliced it till it squeaked.

I knew he wouldn't want me to ask about his disorders. Instead, when I had freed my teeth of suet, I asked, 'You don't really think Tebbit killed himself to avoid a trip abroad, do you?'

'Who knows?' The Major chewed resolutely. 'You can't tell with a chap like that. Never been farther than Shepherd's Bush – never lived, you might say – and now he's dead.' He swallowed his mouthful. 'Ever thought about it?'

'About what?'

'Being dead. I've never fancied it. Not in a coffin six feet down nor fried in a crematorium. Seen the practical equivalent of both too often, during the war. One couldn't afford to go broody in those days, but I often think about it now.'

The Major looked pale in contrast to the beef-fed portraits. And when he glanced over his shoulder at a waitress outflanking him with a tray of treacle pudding, there was a hunted flash of eye-white. He recommended the pudding, but I joined him in settling for coffee. He sipped thoughtfully. 'That girl – what's her name? Perpetua? You know, if she hadn't got across me at the Board meeting that time, I'd never have left and Tebbit would never have come; so he'd never have left and never have gone to the gallery and killed himself. Funny, isn't it?'

'I suppose it is'.

'Yes, well . . . She wasn't a bad sort of girl at bottom. You couldn't really call her fat.'

On the steps outside the Major said he must be off. 'Got to go in for a check-up – did I tell you? And then I'm going live somewhere decent. Somewhere abroad.'

He was singing bravely as he drove off.

ICE DANCING

Rose Tremain

Rose Tremain's novels include *Sadlers Birthday*, *The Swimming Pool Season* and *Restoration* (which was shortlisted for the Booker Prize and won the *Sunday Express* Book of the Year Award). She has published two collections of short stories (*The Colonel's Daughter & Other Stories* won the Dylan Thomas Award in 1984) and written plays for television and radio. Her latest novel is called *Sacred Country*. She lives in Norwich.

'Ice Dancing' was first broadcast on Radio 4, read by Harry Trowb.

ICE DANCING

Let me tell you about our house first. Then I'll talk about us and the kind of people we are.

Our house is in Maryland, USA. Our local town is called Cedar, but we're nine miles from there, out on our own, facing a creek. We call the creek Our Creek and I built our house at the edge of it, with every window looking towards the water.

I'm an architect. Retired now. This was my last big challenge, to arrange this house so that wherever you are in it, you get a glimmer of Our Creek. Janet, my wife, didn't believe I could do this. She said: 'Don, what about the rooms at the back?' I explained to her that there wouldn't *be* any rooms at the back. 'Sweetheart,' I said, 'think of the house as half a necklace and the water as a neck.' The only thing that's at the back of the house is the front door.

Our Creek flows towards the mighty Chesapeake Bay. On summer evenings, Janet and I stand on our jetty, hand in hand, sipping a cocktail and watching the water slide by. Sometimes, we don't talk. We just stand there watching and sipping and not talking. We've been married for thirty-seven years and now here we are with the place of our dreams. I began life as a clerk. Janet began life behind a Revlon counter.

And we've travelled the world. We started life as dumb Americans, but we didn't stay that way. We've been to England and France and Sweden. And Russia. We've got a whole heap of memories of Stockholm and Moscow. In Stockholm, we visited Strindberg's apartment. We saw his bed and his inkstand and his hairbrushes. He used these brushes to fluff out his hair because he was embarrassed about his head. Not many Americans know this, that the great playwright,

175

Strindberg had a tiny little pin head he was ashamed of.

In Moscow, we witnessed a multiple wedding. We were standing in the snow, hand in hand. The doors of a grey building opened and out of them came a stream of brides, arm in arm with their bridegrooms. It was February. Ten degrees below. And the brides were wearing thin dresses of white net and carrying blood-red bouquets. Janet never got over this sight. Years later, we'd be lying in bed and she'd say: 'Remember those Soviet brides, Don? Out in the cold like that.' It upset her somehow.

And yet winter was her favourite season. The year we moved into this house Our Creek froze. We woke up one morning and there it was: all the water normally headed for the bay was frozen stock still. We stood together at our bedroom window, gaping. We were snug in there, on account of the triple glazing I'd had fitted. I put my arm around Janet and held her to me and her body was warm as pie. 'Don,' she whispered. 'let's go out there. Let's go out and dance on the ice.'

I said: 'What d'you mean, dance? We don't have any skates.'

'I don't mean skate,' she said. 'I mean *dance*.'

So that's what we did. We went straight out there before breakfast. We got dressed up in Russian hats and our winter coats and our snow boots. We were sixty years old and we started singing and waltzing on the ice! We sang any old tune that came into our heads, but neither of us has got a voice and we'd forgotten most of the words, so the whole darn thing was crazy. And then, in the middle of it all, as we kept slipping and tripping and laughing, I had this vision of Strindberg. He was standing in the sky, staring down at us. And he wasn't smiling. So I quit laughing and I said to Janet: 'That's enough. Time for breakfast.'

'Oh why, Don? This is *fun*.'

'It's also suicidal. We never thought about that.'

The thing I'll tell you about next happened in Cedar.

Cedar is a smart little Maryland town with three banks

and two churches and an avenue of limes along Main Street. There isn't one single cedar tree in it.

We were on Main Street when this thing happened. I'd been to my bank and Janet had been in the hardware store, buying a hose nozzle. It was a spring morning. The limes were coming into leaf and I stood on the sidewalk looking at Janet about to cross over to me and thinking, here she comes, my Revlon girl.

She walked to the middle of the road and stopped. Then she fell down. She lay in the road. She didn't try to get up.

I ran to her. I could see a truck coming towards us. I put my arms out, waving it down. Other people came running. I knelt down and held onto Janet. Her eyes were open and her face was yellow-white.

'Honey,' I said, 'what happened?'

She held onto me. Her mouth opened and closed, opened and closed, trying to make words, but no words came out.

'OK,' I said, 'it's OK, it's OK . . .'

I sent a boy on a skateboard to call for an ambulance. There was a whole cluster of people round us now. I had to ask them politely to step back, to give Janet some air, to give me room to left up her head.

We got her to the hospital. The doctors were confused. They said: 'It may have been a mild epileptic seizure. We're not sure. We'll do some tests. Meanwhile, she's fine. You can go see her.'

She was pink again and sitting up in bed. She was wearing a hospital gown, tied at the back. She took my hands in hers. She said: 'I'm sorry, honey. I thought I was back in Danesville, that's all.'

Danesville, West Virginia was Janet's old home town. Her dad worked in a glass foundry there. Her mother had raised four children on a foundryman's wage and sent the only girl, Janet, to Beauty School.

After two days, they sent Janet home. They told me at the hospital: 'We can't pinpoint anything at the present time. It isn't epilepsy. Let us know if she has more falls.'

We went home. We had to drive through Cedar, past the exact spot where Janet had fallen down and I knew I would never go by this place without remembering Janet lying in the road. I thought this would be the thing that would trouble me most in the weeks to come.

But the weeks to come were like no other weeks in my whole life. Boy-o-boy.

The Janet I took home from the hospital was the Janet I knew, but right from this day the Janet I knew started to slip away from me. She went back into her past. Not all the time. Sometimes, she was right there with me and we'd play a sensible game of Rummy or do the crossword or go down to the jetty together and listen and watch for signs of spring. And then, without any warning, bang, her mind got up and walked away someplace else. Mainly, it walked to Danesville. She'd say: 'Don, the temperature on the foundry floor is one hundred thirty degrees Fahrenheit. Daily temperatures of this kind burn up a person's life.' Or she'd think our kitchen, with all its built-in appliances, was her mother's old kitchen and she'd complain about soot. She'd say to me, in a simpering voice like her mother's: 'Modern detergents are not designed to cope with old-fashioned problems.'

Sometimes, talking to her would help and sometimes it wouldn't.

Sometimes, if I sat her down and stroked her head and said: 'Janet, you are *not* in Danesville, sweetheart. You are here in the home I built for you, all safe and sound,' she would come out of her trance and say: 'Sure, Don, I know that. You don't need to tell me.'

Then it could happen, too, that she mistook me for one of her brothers. I'd say: 'I am not Charlie, Janet. Charlie was bald, remember? I've got hair like old Strindberg, wild and fluffy.' But she'd refuse to believe me. She'd say: 'You're Charlie. You always were a prankster. And who's Strindberg?'

She got clumsy. She'd always been a meticulous woman. Now, she dropped things and spilled her food and burned her hands on the stove. I said to her one day: 'Janet, I can't stand this any more.' I left the house and went down to the

178

jetty and got into the little canoe we keep tied up there and paddled off down the creek in the rain. I started crying like a baby. I hadn't cried since I was an office clerk.

They operated on Janet on June 30th. It was a hot morning.

Her condition is called hydrocephalus. Water builds up inside the skull and presses on the brain. If the water can't be drained off, parts of the brain atrophy. Then the person slips away – back into the past or to any place where she can't be reached. The success rate of the operation to drain off the water is variable according to age. About thirty per cent of those operated on die.

Death, to me, has always been synonymous with falling. This is how my mind sees it; a long, black, sickening fall. And Janet saw it the same. I once asked her.

Before Janet's operation, the surgeon came to see me. He said: 'Go home. Dig the yard. Mend a fence. This is a long operation. She's in our hands now. There's nothing you can do.'

I said: 'Sure. I understand.'

But I didn't leave. I sat on a chair in a Waiting Area and concentrated my mind on holding Janet up.

I held her in different ways. I carried her above my head, holding her waist and her thigh. When this got tiring, I put her on my back – her back to my back – and her legs made an arc around mine. Then I flew her above me, my hands on her tummy. I stood her on my shoulders and hung onto her feet . . .

People come into the Waiting Area. They looked at magazines. They read the words 'Ford' or 'Toyota' on their car-key tags. They didn't bother me. They recognised that I was busy.

To help me, I sang songs in my mind and I whirled Janet around in time to these. I dressed her in a floaty kind of dress to make her lighter in my imaginary arms. As the hours passed, she got younger. Her hair hung down like it used to when she was a Revlon girl . . .

Then someone spoke to me. It was the surgeon. He seemed

to have learned my first name. 'Donald,' he said, 'I'm pretty sure your wife's going to make it.'

They kept her in hospital quite a long while. Then I took her home and the summer passed and then the fall and now here we are again in the winter and this morning we woke up to find Our Creek covered with ice.

Every day, I watch Janet. I watch and wait, for the least sign that she's slipping back to Danesville, but none comes.

She's in fine spirits, too, keen to do things. She says we should travel again, see more of the world before we leave it.

Today, we dress up warm and go down to the creek and Janet says: 'Come on, Don, look at this great ice! Let's dance and fool around on it like we did before.'

She's at the end of the jetty. She's all ready to climb down onto the frozen water.

But I can see that this ice is pretty thin. It's not like it was in that other winter, two foot thick; it's a different kind of ice.

So I call Janet back. I say: 'Honey, don't go down there. It's too dangerous. Enough dancing already. Right? Just stay up here with me.'

THE INTERVIEW

Maeve Binchy

Maeve Binchy was born in Dublin. She worked as a teacher and later as a journalist for the *Irish Times*. Her stories have been published widely and her bestselling novels, extensively translated, include *Light a Penny Candle*, *Firefly Summer*, *Echoes* and *Circle of Friends*. Her latest *The Copper Beech* was published last autumn.

'The Interview' was first broadcast on Radio 4, read by Kate Binchy.

THE INTERVIEW

She was the youngest, and the pet. Probably she would have been the pet anyway, even if she hadn't been deaf. But once they realised that she would never hear properly the boys became fiercely protective of Bessie. Their only sister, the little toddler with the curls in her eyes. They got used to pushing her hair back so that she could see their faces as they talked.

It became second nature to them to position Bessie with her back to the light. They spoke clearly so that she could lip-read. They didn't playact or pull funny faces to confuse her and they had all developed this semi-automatic habit of touching her lightly on the arm when anyone addressed a question to her, so that she would look up and pay attention.

They were tough boys, the Ryan lads. You didn't cross them lightly. Not if you wanted a peaceful life. They more or less ran things at school, all three of them in their different worlds. Kenny Ryan who got fellows into pool halls long before they were old enough, through some kind of system of tidying up and keeping their mouths shut. And there was Frank Ryan who was Mr Football, and Lar who played with a group. All right, so they were only ten years old, but people had to start somewhere.

And nobody outside the door of Number 46 Wattle Street would have known that the three tough Ryan boys were like pussycats when it came to looking after their little sister.

Bessie with the huge bright eyes and the golden curls was the one who could make them do anything.

'You're making too much noise,' she would say to Lar.

'You can't hear whether we are or not.' Lar was spirited.

183

'No, but I can see Mam and Dad put their hands over their ears.' Bessie missed nothing.

Bessie would warn Frank that it was the mud being walked into the house that annoyed their parents, not the fact that he played football. And she could tell Kenny that they didn't worry about the billiards or snooker, it was just the thought of the kids drinking up there that caused the fuss.

By the time she was seven Bessie Ryan ran the house. There was greater peace in Number 46 than in many another in Wattle Street. None of the neighbours considered that it was any handicap for Bessie being deaf. Where was the handicap they asked?

And Bessie's brothers didn't think of it as a lack. Their sister was more alert than anyone in the house.

Once, some friend of Frank's misguidedly called her a deaf dummy, and the bruises he got didn't die down for weeks. But Bessie's mother and father worried. They never talked about it in front of her since they knew she was aware of every nuance and glance that went between them. Sometimes she would ask them. 'Are you talking about me?' And she would touch her ears and lips as if she knew they thought it a problem. They were quick to lie and assure her that they weren't. Then it seemed better to let her in on it. She would guess anyway. There were so many things they worried about.

They didn't want her to ride a bicycle up and down Wattle Street like the other children. They could hear the angry hoots and toots of the cars and the trucks that came around corners at dangerous speeds. Bessie wouldn't be able to hear that.

They worried when they took her to the sea. She couldn't hear the shouts of the lifeguard. They felt sad when they saw her watching the pop stars that the other seven year olds would sing along with. Bessie would never hear the music.

'I can know the words,' she said once to reassure them.

'Lord! You'd be better not knowing the words,' said her father. Timmy Ryan hadn't much time for modern music.

Mary Ryan knew that if there was to be a good life for her beautiful daughter it couldn't be lived out in Wattle Street. If

Bessie grew up here, she would end up an indulged and partially educated girl.

At school they would be kind to her. The teachers would do their best, but there was nobody trained to teach a deaf child. There would be none of the specialised skills she needed. Bessie would grow up, over-protected at home, and at school sitting in a classroom where much would pass her by. She might learn keyboard skills but would there be anyone who could make her mind leap and soar the way it deserved to.

Mary Ryan only spoke of it when the bedroom door was closed behind them. 'We have to give her the best chance there is,' she said over and over, persuading herself as well as Timmy.

Her husband knew his role. He had to put up the arguments against sending Bessie away to a school which would equip her for a better life. 'It's too early to be thinking about it. She's only seven and a bit.' That was one ploy.

'They take them from seven.' That was the answer. They both knew it.

'If we want her to live in the real world with deaf people and hearing people then why should we send her out of the real world?' He was hopeful, but not very.

They both knew why.

This was one of the best schools that anyone had ever heard of. People from everywhere tried to get in. It was a hundred miles away. The Principal was a magic kind of woman. She assumed that there was nothing a deaf girl couldn't do. Her past pupils were all over the world, unaffected by their lack of hearing, confident and happy.

'We would never be able to afford the fees.' Timmy said this often, even though he knew that Mary would see the fees were not relevant. If a child was bright and could benefit from the school the fees were found.

There were only two real arguments.

Timmy always left those to the end.

'We'd miss her terribly. It's miles away.'

'But that would be pure selfishness if we put that before doing the best for her,' Mary replied.

And then the crunch one.

'Would she get in?'

That was the one they didn't know the answer to.

Perhaps Bessie Ryan with the intelligent eyes, and the ready understanding was NOT as bright as they thought. Maybe they found her superintelligent because she was so adored.

The only girl. The baby of the family. The beautiful child.

Perhaps when she went off to the school, the place with the rolling green fields where the girls learned every sport . . . she wouldn't seem bright by comparison.

Something in Mary and Timmy Ryan didn't want to believe that either. Even though it was the perfect excuse if they didn't want to lose her. They could always say that they had tried but it hadn't worked. That they had done everything they could to get her in but it had proved impossible. But Bessie must triumph. That was a higher law than anything. So they stopped talking behind closed doors. They took her into their confidence. She didn't cry or cling, or refuse to go.

She regarded it as a competition. A hurdle to be leaped.

'It would be nice for you too, as you're getting old and grey,' she said consolingly to her parents.

'Well, that won't be for some time yet,' Mary Ryan bridled.

'Not old and grey exactly,' her father explained.

'But you are old. You're in your forties,' Bessie said. 'You'd be worried in case you dropped dead from age and what would happen to me when you're dead and gone.'

Mary Ryan knew it was better to go along with her daughter's wilder attitudes to things.

'Yes well. Of course, that's a point, but your brothers would always look after you.'

'They'll probably marry awful mad people like themselves,' Bessie said after some thought. 'No, I'd say you're right. The best thing is to try and get me into this school place. I can come home some weekends, can't I?'

So now it was all in the open. The need for the staged conversations in the bedroom was over. Bessie Ryan was

going to give it her best shot. She was going to get into this
school which would train her for a better life.

They made enquiries. It would involve an interview. The
girls were accepted or rejected on a personal meeting with Win.

Her name was Sister Winifred. She had been a nun in
Community once. But now she didn't wear the habit of a
religious order. No one was quite sure whether she was still
a nun or not. She had the burning zeal and enthusiasm that
some would associate with being part of a religious order.
She was single and lived in almost monastic simplicity. Yet
she drove a sports car and fraternised with politicians and
captains of industry in order to raise funding for her work.
She had penetrating eyes. People said she looked as if she
could see straight into their souls.

Mary and Timmy Ryan went to see her first on their own.
Win liked that. She wanted to hear directly about the family
background without having the child present. Sometimes she
learned enough about the child from the talk with parents to
decide whether or not there would be a vacancy.

But she always saw the little deaf girl, whoever she
was.

She would give advice and she would make suggestions.
She never apologised for not being able to take every single
applicant in. Win was a realist. She knew that only so much
could be done. Not any more.

Win liked the Ryans. They told her without any sense of
vanity of the child's beauty, and how her face lit up when
she understood things. Win had seen this many times in deaf
children, but she didn't feel it necessary to spoil Timmy and
Mary Ryan's delight in their own little girl. They told how
Bessie could name every bird that landed on the bird table,
and how they played draughts every night, and wished there
was someone who could teach her chess.

'That's very bright for a child not yet eight, isn't it Sister
Win?' Mary Ryan had her knuckles clenched in hope for her
daughter.

Win remained calm: 'Yes, of course it is. But we'll wait

and see, shall we? Let's see how Bessie gets on when she comes here.'

The boys didn't want Bessie to go.

'There's going to be fights when you're not in the house,' said Lar.

'That's because you'll be causing them,' Bessie replied.

'Who'll stand up for me to Mam?' Frank asked.

'I tell you, it's a matter of not bringing in a load of mud.' Bessie was amazed he couldn't see it.

'We'll forget you, you'll forget us.' Kenny was so gloomy about it all.

'Not if you ever come home from the pool hall. I'll be home a lot of weekends.'

They knew she wanted it now, so they tried to help her for the Test.

'You'll probably be asked about the pop groups and chart toppers,' Lar said, and gave her long lessons for contingencies.

'They might ask you about the league.' Frank had all the details.

Kenny said it was more likely to be general knowledge, and looked up facts about the speed of light and the circumference of the earth.

On the morning of the interview they were all very nervous.

'It won't matter if you don't get in,' Kenny said. 'There'll always be a job for you up in the pool hall after they're dead and gone.' He indicated his parents with a nod of his head.

'You tell them you know all about relegation and they'll let you in,' Frank advised.

'Maybe we should have done a bit of opera, heavy stuff.' Lar was doubtful.

'She'll be fine,' said her father with a shaky voice.

'A school that won't take Bessie isn't a real school,' said Mary Ryan in a wavering tone.

The interview seemed to be going very well.

Win gave her a lot of tests. She started speaking with her

back to the child and then continued the conversation face to face.

'I'm sorry, I missed what you said when I couldn't see your face,' Bessie said.

There was a nod of approval.

Mary clutched her husband's hand. Bessie was doing her stuff. She was showing how an education like this would never be wasted on her.

They walked the grounds of the school.

Bessie asked interested questions about the hockey pitch and netball courts. 'I know a lot about soccer,' she confided to Win. 'You know, when to take a corner, and when it's a free kick. I learned it just in case . . .' Her voice trailed away, as if she had seen the futility of it.

But Win seemed to be nodding with approval.

They went to the room with the loose reverberating floorboards, where the girls learned to dance by feeling the rhythm.

'Isn't that very interesting!' Bessie said. 'I never thought we'd be able to dance. I know a lot about pop music though . . . I learned it just in case . . .' Again her voice died away. As if she saw that the received wisdom from her brothers might not have been all that helpful.

Then they all came back to Win's study.

This was a simple intelligence test. It was a matter of simple arithmetic, subtraction and division on little cards. Well within her grasp.

And something almost too simple. Identifying objects.

Win looked at her as Bessie clearly acknowledged the drawing with the floppy ears and the round tail was a rabbit, and the one with the long tail and the whiskers was a cat. She did a house, a boat and an aeroplane.

All on cards.

Mary and Timmy Ryan sat there, sides touching.

Mary thought about the parents who must have come in here and hoped and prayed and seen their child stumble and be unsure. Timmy wondered what the house would be like without his daughter. He knew he must be strong and delighted for her success. She, without hearing, would achieve more than any of her brothers who could hear the grass grow.

Then they saw her pause over a drawing.

It was a slice of cheese, a triangular piece. As obvious as anything.

Four years ago when she was only three and a bit she could have recognised cheese.

Bessie was turning the card upside down. She was looking at it puzzled.

Win told her . . . take your time.

The bright face was screwed up in a struggle to understand. She held it at every angle, but still she could make neither head nor tail of it.

'No idea at all?' Win sounded puzzled too, and disappointed.

'Please God may she say it. May she say the word cheese,' Mary prayed. 'It can't matter to you God much, but it matters to us all, and to Bessie. Let her know it's cheese.'

Timmy's nails were in his palms.

Perhaps this was meant to happen. Maybe she was meant to stay at home with them. Perhaps the little monkey was even doing it deliberately.

But Bessie's face was red with exertion. She looked from one to another.

Win's face was impassive, her mother's staring trying not to hint the word, not to mouth it to her as a cheat.

'I don't know. I really don't know I'm afraid.' She shook her golden curls sadly. She knew she was letting them down.

'No idea at all, Bessie? You've done so well on all the others.' Win wasn't pressuring her, but trying to keep it open all the same.

'No.'

'Have a guess. Often guesses work.'

Bessie looked long and hard. The lines were so simple, it was so hard to tell, there were no hints in the picture.

Well, the woman had told her to guess. She might as well guess. It could be right, and if not well she was out anyway.

'Would it be Caerphilly?'

The Interview

Bessie was very bright but she didn't understand why three pairs of eyes filled with tears. She knew many brands of cheese and assumed she was meant to pick the right one.

And she looked around from one to the other and knew, despite the sudden and unexpected burst of emotion, that she was in to the school.

Hadn't she been lucky to think of the right cheese. There had been so many to choose from.

TELLING STORIES

Russell Hoban

Russell Hoban, born in Pennsylvania, has lived in London since 1969. Many of his stories are in the collection *The Moment under the Moment*. His novels include *Riddley Walker*, *Pilgermann*, and *The Medusa Frequency*. 'The Second Mrs Kong,' an opera collaboration with Harrison Birtwistle, will have its first performance at Glyndebourne in 1994.

'Telling Stories' was first broadcast on Radio 3, read by Joss Ackland.

TELLING STORIES

I wonder if this happens to a lot of men. You've been married for a certain length of time, twenty years maybe, or thirty. You're not as young as you used to be, you've put on weight and somehow food seems to land on the front of you when you're eating. Your wife never fails to notice that but you can't always get her attention at other times. Actually I'm talking about my wife, not yours. I mean, I'd come into the kitchen – that's where she did her newspaper reading, and she did more and more of that as time went on – and I'd say, 'I got a really good start on the new chapter this afternoon: *Vermeer and the Golden Age of Dutch Painting.*'

'Mmm,' she'd say, not lifting her head from the paper.

At bedtime she'd stretch and yawn so hugely that I thought she'd dislocate her jaw. 'One less day to get through!' she'd say. She'd kept her looks though. She was a handsome woman and always very well-groomed: a smart dresser with a face and figure that still made men look twice.

I've always been a night owl; some of my best ideas have come at two and three in the morning. It used to be that we'd go to bed together at a reasonable hour and then maybe later I'd come down to my desk and do some work. After a while, though, I got into the habit of working straight on while she went off to bed. I'd carry on till midnight or one o'clock, then I'd watch a late film or a video till half-past two or three.

My TV life wasn't entirely solitary. There were certain programmes we always watched together – *LA Law* for example. But more and more she liked things like *Last of the Summer Wine* and *M*A*S*H* and *Inspector Morse* and *The Ruth Rendell Mysteries* while I preferred Stephen King films and Hammer Horror and science fiction like *Blade Runner* or *Dreamscape* as well as some of those Channel 4 efforts that are high on nudity and low on plot. Now and then there'd be a good straight film that she simply didn't want to stay up for so I'd tell her the story of it the next day – not in the morning, we had the *Times* and the *Guardian* to get through and we never talked much then, but in the afternoon when I'd come down to the kitchen for a coffee.

'I watched *Born in East LA* last night,' I said to her one day. 'Funniest thing I've ever seen. There was this really charming little Hispanic guy with a big moustache, sweet guy, he's a car mechanic, lives with his mother and his sister in LA which is where he was born. He's a third-generation American. At the start of the film we see him at breakfast and his mother has this big photographic picture of Jesus in a fancy frame: one of those pictures they laminate in such a way that when you turn your head his eyes open and close.' And my wife's eyes – her name is Gloria actually – her eyes got all bright and she was really looking at me, smiling and all excited and laughing already, really interested and actually hanging on my words as I went on with the story: 'They have their telephone in a little niche in the dining-room and she props up this Jesus picture so it covers up the telephone. OK, so now the mother and the sister have to go to Fresno but the mother tells Rudy – that's this little guy's name – to pick up his cousin Xavier who's arriving from Mexico illegally and doesn't speak a word of English. He's never seen Xavier so she gives him a photo and he's to go to this toy factory where Xavier's going to turn up. The entire factory staff are illegal immigrants, OK? So the mother and the sister are gone now and Rudy's off in his little pink VW convertible to meet Xavier but he forgets his wallet with all his ID in it. He leaves it on the table or whatever and off he goes . . .'

The way she looked at me when I told her the story of that film! I hadn't had that kind of a response for ten or fifteen years and about two or three stone. It made me feel that I wasn't altogether invisible, that I might actually cast a shadow and have a reflection in a mirror.

So I'd always look at the TV programmes in the paper first

thing in the morning and I'd plan my tapings for the day and night. We only had one video-recorder at first but all too often there'd be two good films on at the same time . . . So I hired a second video-recorder and then a third one in order to stay on top of the situation. No *double entendre* intended but I have to say that things between us got a little more intimate as the afternoon story sessions went on. I suppose storytellers way back living in caves had groupies; there's a real power in being able to hold a listener.

The films I told her! – *Murder C.O.D.*; *Innerspace*; *Stakeout*; *Big*; *The Burbs* and many, many more. It got to be a regular part of the day. I was high on telling film stories and this new responsiveness from Gloria, I was feeling really up – twenty years younger and two stone lighter and no food down my front. Sometimes I'd suggest that we watch, together, one of the films I'd told her about, I never mind seeing a good picture twice; I guess I've seen *Blade Runner* and *The Philadelphia Experiment* four or five times. And *Blowout*! seven times at least: I always like Nancy Allen. But Gloria never wanted to see the film once she'd heard the story. Life was too short, she said, and the story was enough.

As time went on, however, I began to wonder about the whole thing. I mean, I was the medium but I certainly wasn't the message. She was looking at me but she was seeing William Devane or Dennis Quaid or Richard Dreyfuss or Tom Hanks . . .

One morning Gloria said to me, 'Well, did you watch anything good last night?'

'Mmm,' I said. 'An old Burt Lancaster film from 1966 – *Profit and Loss.*'

'I like Burt Lancaster,' she said, 'but I don't think I've ever seen that one.'

'In this picture he's an accountant. A colourless sort of man with bi-focals, in his fifties maybe. The children have grown up and left home and it's just him and his wife, Kim Hunter. They hardly look at each other any more except when she brushes the dandruff off his suit before he leaves for work.

She's not a bad-looking woman, quite a good-looking woman actually – well, you've seen Kim Hunter . . .'

'I'm not sure I remember her,' said Gloria. 'What kind of hair does she have?'

'Brown.'

'How does she do it?'

'Short, with a parting and it's sort of wavy. She's kind of prim but sexy with it and a nice little figure. And Burt Lancaster of course is Burt Lancaster. But they just don't see each other as people any more. She reads thrillers and romances and he brings home work from the office and they have their regular domestic routine and when they go upstairs at night it's Horlicks and a book in bed.'

'It was an American film, wasn't it?' said Gloria. 'Do they have Horlicks in America?'

'Did I say Horlicks? It might have been Ovaltine.'

'What did they read?'

'He read *New Horizons in Inheritance Tax* and she read some kind of bodice-ripper. I don't remember the title.'

'How old was Burt Lancaster in real life when the film was made?'

'Fifties, mid-fifties I'd say. Just old enough for the kids to have gone off to university. One evening he's going through the household accounts when he finds a slip of paper with her handwriting on it. It's an ad for the personal columns: "Middle-aged woman, fond of books, music, seeks correspondent for exchange of thoughts."'

'I think I know what's going to happen,' said Gloria. 'He starts writing to her?'

'You got it. He starts writing to her under an assumed name.'

'Doesn't she recognise his handwriting?'

'He types his letters at the office. You see him sitting there after everyone's gone home. The lights of the city are on and he's all alone in the office except for the cleaning ladies, all alone with the light of the desk lamp on the letter as it comes out of the typewriter: "Dear Gwendolyn," he types . . .'

'She told her name in the ad?'

'This is already his second letter we're seeing. I forgot to say that we've seen her getting a stack of letters from the newspaper box number and she picks out his to answer. So we've seen him get her first letter as well. And Gwendolyn isn't her real name, it's Grace. "Dear Gwendolyn," he types . . .'

'Was this in black and white or colour?'

'It was in colour, so we're seeing the colour of the night sky outside the windows and the city lights and the cars and the illuminated signs. There's a lot of mood in this, a lot of atmosphere. It's a very sensitive film. "Dear Gwendolyn," he types, "For such a very long time I've had no one to exchange thoughts with – they've all been chasing one another around in my head and getting mixed up with the empty numbers that my life has become."'

'But a man like Burt Lancaster,' said Gloria, 'surely finding a woman to exhange thoughts with is no problem for him?'

'He's not the sort of man who runs around; he's a serious type and he's just sort of withdrawn into himself over the years. He wouldn't know how to approach a new woman any more.'

'And yet it's so much easier for a man. A woman, when she's young she can make things happen. But when you get a little older you're lucky if they stop for you at a zebra crossing.'

'Well, they're both in the same boat then because nobody's been stopping for him either. As a matter of fact there's a scene where he's hurrying to post a letter and he almost gets knocked down by a car.'

'Serves him right.'

'What do you mean? What's he done that he deserves to be hit by a car?'

'What's he done? It's what he hasn't done! When was the last time he took her out for a meal or to the theatre or even just for a walk? Work, work, work. That's all he does and what's the good of it? So she's got a roof over her head: that's what she's got out of life at the age of fifty-something – a roof over her head. Are you surprised that she's looking for

199

someone to communicate with, to bring a little not even excitement, just a little relief from every day being the same and full of emptiness?'

'And what do you think it's been for him?' I said. 'Riotous living and dining and dancing and partying every night? And now he's no longer young and there are twenty-year-old accountants coming up all the time, willing to do his job for less money. Any day he could be out on the street and who'll want him at his age? So it's not easy for him either.'

'It's an escape from reality for both of them,' said Gloria.

'Or into it. The life of the mind is also part of reality.'

'So anyhow, what happened?'

'The letters go back and forth and we see a lot of each of them alone and we feel how they're trying to reach out for what's gone out of their lives. Finally she writes to him that maybe they ought to meet.'

'She makes the first move!'

'She makes the first move and he decides to chance it.'

'Has he been using his real name?'

'No, he's been calling himself John. His real name is Harold. They both make up excuses for an evening out: she says she's going for dinner with a woman friend she knew at university and he says he's got to help the boss entertain a client from Saudi Arabia. There's a very touching sequence where the camera goes back and forth between the two of them as they get ready. You know, she's standing in front of the mirror trying on different dresses and putting on perfume and all that and he's dousing himself with aftershave and making sure he hasn't got dandruff on his shoulders and he goes out and buys flowers . . .'

'Where are they meeting?'

'It's a place called *Chez Antoine*, it's a restaurant where he used to go years ago before he was married.'

'So what's she going to do with flowers in a restaurant?'

'I don't know, he didn't think of that. There would have been a touching little scene with the waiter getting a vase and so on.'

'What do you mean, "would have been"?'

'He's rushing to the restaurant on foot, she's driving there in her car; he crosses the street without looking and Bam!'

'O my God! She hit him?'

'With a Volvo estate.'

'Is he dead?'

'Almost. He's lying there looking up at her and she's kneeling beside him cradling his head in her arms and he says, "Gwendolyn" and then he's gone. She's kneeling there in the rain with the traffic all around her and drivers blowing their horns and then they freeze frame and we see the credits rolling.'

Gloria had tears running down her face and I took her in my arms and we went upstairs. Actually there never was a Burt Lancaster film called *Profit and Loss*. Not that I'd ever heard of, at any rate. It was *The Lair of the White Worm* that I'd watched the night before but I don't think I'd have got the same result with that one.

After that I made up a lot of films and I got better and better at it and the afternoons and evenings got a lot livelier. Little by little I made the male lead less good-looking and more like real life. He kept getting more and more overweight and closer to sixty than fifty and he sometimes had food down his front and dandruff on his shoulders. Finally I made up a film with Sydney Greenstreet as an art historian and Glynis Johns as a museum curator who falls in love with him. That one had a lot of art in it but perhaps it lacked the dramatic inevitability of some of my other inventions. I noticed half-way through that Gloria was yawning.

'Tired?' I said.

She was looking at me with a very hard face. 'What did you say the title of this film was?'

'*The Fake*.'

'Glynis Johns and Sydney Greenstreet! Have you still got the tape?'

'No, I recorded *Nightmare on Elm Street* over it.'

'Liar.'

'What do you mean?'

201

'The Sydney Greenstreet character in the film is remarkably like you, wouldn't you say?'

'Well, you know what they say about life imitating art.'

'Rubbish. You made up that story. There never was such a film.'

'All right,' I said, 'I made it up. Gwendolyn.'

I thought we could freeze frame and roll the credits then. But I was wrong: a week later Gloria ran off with a man she'd been corresponding with unbeknownst to me. Forty-two years old. I wouldn't have minded so much if he'd been some kind of intellectual but he's a car mechanic. End of story.

DUNCAN MINSHULL

TELLING STORIES
The Best of BBC Radio's Recent Short Fiction

In this first collection of short stories commissioned by BBC Radio 3 and Radio 4, established writers are offset by memorable new talent with pieces chosen, as in the second volume, for their striking quality, originality and absorbing narratives.

'There's a whole world in these stories'
Natalie Wheen on Kaleidoscope

A. L. Barker	Maeve Binchy
Christopher Burns	Michael Carson
Angela Carter	Mary Flanagan
Jane Gardam	Romesh Gunesekera
Christopher Hope	John McGahern
Deborah Moggach	Richard Nelson
Frederic Raphael	Michele Roberts
Dilys Rose	Greg Snow
D. J. Taylor	Jonathan Treitel
Lynne Truss	

CORONET BOOKS

MAEVE BINCHY

CIRCLE OF FRIENDS

'Binchy's novels are never less than entertaining, they are, without exception repositories of common sense and good humour, chronicled with tenderness and wit'
The Sunday Times

An enchanting novel of fierce loyalty and love in changing times.

Big generous-hearted Benny and the elfin Eve Malone have been best friends throughout their childhoods in sleepy Knockglen. When the two girls go to study in Dublin, they meet a circle of friends that includes handsome Jack Foley and the selfish but beautiful Nan Mahon – whose ambitions will drag them all into trouble.

As Knockglen is surprised into new life, Benny and Eve discover that among the many distractions of growing up true friendship is the greatest gift of all.

CORONET BOOKS

Ed. DAVID MARCUS

STATE OF THE ART

Since early this century, Irish writers have been acclaimed world-wide for their short stories. But the traditional themes of such celebrated past masters as James Joyce and Liam O'Flaherty no longer hold centre stage. From the 1960s onwards, feminism and other fundamental social changes have created fresh ground for a new generation of Irish writers. This selection of their richly varied, stimulating and entertaining short stories displays the flourishing state of the art in Ireland today.

'Thirty-four excellent stories'
The Sunday Times

John Banville	Maeve Kelly
Maeve Binchy	Rita Kelly
Clare Boylan	Adrian Kenny
Helen Lucy Burke	Mary Leland
Evelyn Conlon	Bernard MacLaverty
Shane Connaughton	Seán MacMathúna
Emma Cooke	Aidan Mathews
Ita Daly	John Morrow
Anne Devlin	Éilis Ní Dhuibhne
Mary Dorcey	Gillman Noonan
Anne Enright	Kate Cruise O'Brien
Dermot Healy	Mary O'Donnell
Desmond Hogan	Brian Power
Peter Hollywood	Ronan Sheehan
Neil Jordan	Eddie Stack
John B. Keane	Eithne Strong
Sam Keery	Maura Treacy

SCEPTRE

ROSE TREMAIN

THE GARDEN OF THE VILLA MOLLINI

'The stories have a strange, fairy-tale quality: the simple,
beautiful prose, the sense of inevitability, the use of
allusion and metaphor to suggest undercurrents of
disturbing portent'
Selina Hastings in The Daily Telegraph

'Her talent at its best'
Susan Hill

'Professional, ingenious . . . genuinely witty'
Martin Seymour-Smith in the Financial Times

'A quintessentially English writer – her work has a charm and
finesse, a civilised irony'
Robert Nye in The Guardian

'Talented to the point of rare originality'
Jill Neville in The Independent

'An expert at conveying the kind of apparently inconsequential
detail that might be the moment of definition in someone's life'
The Times Literary Supplement

'A skilled writer deftly turning her hand to different situations'
Vogue

'A collection full of gems'
Country Life

SCEPTRE

RONALD FRAME

WALKING MY MISTRESS IN DEAUVILLE

Comprising a novella and nine short stories, this sparkling collection explores relationships between the sexes from a variety of often surprising angles. From the first awkward sexual awareness of youth to the ritual dances of courtship and the delicate betrayals of marriage, Ronald Frame lets no shade of emotion or sign of deception escape his razor-sharp, playful eye.

'As always, Frame offers masterful subtlety in his plots and characterisation, and varies his vantage point ingeniously'
The Daily Telegraph

'Clearly the work of an author developing into practised maturity . . . his ability to represent a wide range of characters, of either sex, is prodigious'
The Guardian

'The novella is gripping, the best piece of narrative that Mr Frame has written . . . He perpetually brings you up against the otherness of other people, their ultimate unknowability. He renders the surface of life with fascination, because the surface is there to ward off intimacy'
The Scotsman

'It is good to see Ronald Frame in such fine form . . . the cumulative effect is exhilarating'
Scotland on Sunday

'Mr Frame comes to us with a formidable array of gifts . . . His is a literature of nuance, niceties and fine distinction, of subtleties and refined psychological observation'
Glasgow Herald

Publication in Sceptre, July 1993

SCEPTRE

FRANK RONAN

THE BETTER ANGEL

At seventeen, John G. Moore was in need of salvation. Afraid of the dark and of inheriting his mother's madness, he found irresistible the arrogant assurance of a newcomer to his Irish country school – the eccentric Godfrey Temple. Then John G. began to notice the cracks in Temple's patina. Tracing their volatile, doomed friendship, this powerful narrative captures the wit and anarchy of youth and the often painful transition to maturity.

'As exceptional as its predecessors . . . Ronan is as gifted as anyone from his generation, probably even from the next one up. His prose, understated and fluid, provides consistent and enormous pleasure; his exposures of the human heart are performed with a surgeon's skill and patience'
The Sunday Times

'Excellent . . . something of an Irish LE GRAND MEAULNES'
GQ

'Written in a limpid precise style that's resonant but never overwhelming . . . Ronan paints the understated anguish of his characters with wit . . . A mesmerising rites-of-passage story'
Time Out

'Marked by an eloquent and generally taut style . . . Ronan is excellent in tracing the relationship between the awkward and late-developing John G. Moore and the friend he hero-worships'
The Sunday Tribune

SCEPTRE